also by eleanor wells

All Our Yesterdays

This Time Tomorrow

i've been here before

and other stories

eleanor wells

Pumpkin Carriage Press

This is a work of fiction. Any resemblance between original characters and real persons, living or dead, is coincidental.

No part of this book may be reproduced in any form or by any electronic or mechanical means, including information storage and retrieval systems, without written permission from the author, except for the use of brief quotations in a book review.

Copyright © 2026 Eleanor Wells

FIRST EDITION

"The End of All Things," "Fragments of Another Life," "Our Lifelong Dreams," "The Game of Life," and "I've Been Here Before" were previously published in 2025.

Library of Congress Control Number: 2025926386

Ebook ISBN: 979-8-9941888-0-4
Hardcover ISBN: 979-8-9941888-1-1
Paperback ISBN: 979-8-9990404-9-7

Edited by Olivia Bennett
Layout by Vellum

Printed in the United States of America by Pumpkin Carriage Press, an imprint of Cinderella Pictures LLC, Boulder, Colorado.

Cover Art by Eleanor Wells
Colorful Abstract Portrait Painting by Truecreatives sourced from Canva

disclaimer

The following stories contain depictions of grooming, sexual assault and the death of children that some may find upsetting. Reader discretion is advised.

To my grandparents: the two I love and the two I never knew.

Two roads diverged in a wood, and I—
    I took the one less traveled by,
    And that has made all the difference.

— Robert Frost

contents

The End of All Things	1
Fragments of Another Life	13
Our Lifelong Dreams	38
The Game of Life	64
I've Been Here Before	77
Acknowledgments	119
About the Author	121

the end of all things

EMMA ALWAYS LOVED THE SUN. Even in the dead of winter, it could trick you into thinking it was summer just from the way the sunlight reflected through the windows. Her favorite season was early spring, in that brief stretch of time when she first started to feel the darkness and cold chip away little by little until one day, it broke. You would feel it in the air. Things were about to come alive again. The promise of summer was not far away.

In 2017, that day occurred on the last Saturday of February, when she and Hanna were at her grandparents' farm. It was afternoon, the first day above freezing in over a month. They'd sent the girls on a quest to sap maple. Emma was carrying the spile and Hanna, the bucket. Dressed in only a turtleneck sweater, jeans, and a light puffer jacket rather than the layers upon layers she'd become used to was exciting. In every one of her seventeen years living in Vermont, she always seemed to forget that winter wasn't forever.

They were almost to the stretch of trees when Emma heard a chirping bird. She abruptly stopped and smiled.

"Earth to Emma," Hanna said after a beat.

"Sorry," she said. "Spring is here!"

Hanna shrugged. "Yeah…"

"What's wrong?"

"Nothing, it's just, I don't like the heat," Hanna said.

"And I don't like winter."

"The figure skater that hates winter," Hanna remarked. "Where did we find you again?"

"You've always known this about me," Emma said as the two approached a tree. "You act like you're not going to Utah in a week…. so…."

Hanna's face tightened. "You should be coming with us."

Emma shrugged. "Come on, we all know that you're going to be the one in the Olympics and I'm going to be watching on TV in my pajamas."

Hanna closed her mouth as quickly as she opened it.

Her friend was like this. Always dancing around the fact that she was the star.

Emma wasn't jealous. She liked skating, loved it, even. But it wasn't her life the way it was for Hanna. "Besides, I'm doing the play."

"That's right, Glinda," Hanna whispered, casting her gaze downward.

"Actually, in *Wicked*, it's Galinda," Emma playfully corrected.

IN 2022, it also happened on the last Saturday of February, but under very different circumstances. She was lying in her childhood bedroom as the sun flooded through the white curtain over her window, reminding her that brighter, sunnier days, ones that lasted until 9:00 p.m., were ahead.

She was staring at her phone, at the text from a week earlier that brought her back here.

> Hey, Emma. How are you? It's Jason Fink. Is this still your phone number? I ran into your mom and she said you're living in NYC these days. Hopefully you've kept up with skating.

Receiving the text, she'd been surprised. She'd seen it first on her fifteen minute break at work. Why was Hanna's dad texting her out of the blue after five years? She was still thinking about how to reply when she got off and saw he'd texted again.

> Please call me when you get a moment. Thx!

He'd explained everything to her on the phone. The memorial—a gold plaque with Hanna in the midst of skating glory and Vanessa proudly watching. It would hang in the atrium, greeting people right before they entered the rink.

"That sounds really nice," Emma said.

"It's beautiful," Jason replied. "Don't ask how much it

was. I know you don't care, but there's a reason it took five years. Anyways, we're doing a ceremony next week, and um… would you want to say a few words about her?"

"Me? Are you sure?" There had to have been a million people better suited to that task. Emma was only a small blip in the radar of Hanna's life, anyways. That became more and more apparent as she kept winning competitions and Emma fell further and further behind. By the time they'd sapped maple that spring of their senior year, the Olympics were an inevitability for Hanna Fink. Soon, she'd be on to a future brighter than one Cordova, Vermont could ever offer them.

"I'm not going to ask anyone else."

EMMA PUT HER PHONE ASIDE. Her stomach was a rat's nest. She'd written and rewritten the beginning of a speech about fifty times before deciding she was just going to wing it. She was nervous about facing everyone she used to know and fielding questions about why she'd quit even though it was obvious they never really wanted her. There'd been a simple, unbridled joy she'd found in skating when she was young. Competing seemed to tear away at that.

Emma joined the Cordova Skating Club at the start of eighth grade. She'd avoided Hanna at first—being the daughter of the two coaches screamed favoritism—but there was one day, about a week in.

They were all practicing double axels to a mystical

instrumental composition that Emma thought was very beautiful.

She'd fallen flat on her butt for everyone to see.

"Oof, that's going to leave a mark," Hanna said, skating to her. "Are you okay?"

Emma shook her head.

"Hey, Mom, Dad, I'm going to take her to first aid," Hanna told Vanessa and Jason.

"Alright," they said.

"Can you walk?" Hanna asked as they exited the rink and put on their guards.

Emma nodded. As they walked over, she asked what the music was.

"It's *The Lord of the Rings*," she said. "Have you never seen it?"

"No. I don't watch many movies," Emma replied.

"Oh, girl, that's got to change," Hanna said. "They're so good. My favorite character is Éowyn, and when I'm in the Olympics one day, I'm going to dress like her and do a routine to this music."

In the end, she was just bruised. By the time they were back on the rink, they'd made plans to have a sleepover to watch all three. The extended editions, of course.

From then on, nothing could keep them apart.

Emma couldn't help but smile as she thought of the memory. Another one came into her mind. Their last text exchange.

OLYMPIC TRIALS BBY!!!!

OMG

!!!!!!

IM SO PROUD OF U 🛬✈️🧳

SEE U SOON BABE 🍁🍂

The next morning, the news came up on her phone screen.

Plane Crash... No Survivors...

Still lying in her bed, Emma wiped a tear from her eye and gathered all of her courage with a deep breath. It was just after three. She didn't have to be there until six. And it was Saturday. That meant the rink was open to the public.

She got up, dressed in sweats and a fleece, packing a change of clothes for later.

Her parents were in the living room.

"I'm heading over," Emma said. "See you there?"

"You sure, sweetie?" her dad said.

Emma nodded.

"Take my car," her mom told her.

Emma got the keys to the old brown Focus from off its hook.

SHE HADN'T BEEN to the rink since those awful few days after Hanna and Vanessa died. As she pulled into a parking spot, it was like traveling back in time.

It was busy, though probably just because it was Saturday and not what was happening later. Five years on, most people at the rink never knew Hanna or her mother.

Five years was an eternity in the life of a young person, in any case.

She had to pay for a skate rental, something she hadn't done since she was younger than ten years old. The woman at the booth gave her a vaguely condescending smile, as if assuming it was her first time. She had to add an extra $2 for the guards, and $1 for a locker to hold her stuff.

Emma found her way to an empty bench, hesitating as she watched the people around her. It was mostly kids whose parents were trying to keep them still as they tied their laces. Her hands were shaking so badly that she had to start over. She got distracted by a blue tarp covering what was clearly the plaque. Chairs and a podium were set up. Would she really be there in just a few hours? She tried not to think of it.

She messed up on the laces again. What was so hard about this? It's not like she'd done it a million times before. Finally, she got it. They weren't perfect, but they'd stay on her feet, and that's what mattered.

She felt a chill as she walked onto the rink, and not just because of the decrease in temperature. She remembered that she didn't like sharing the rink with so many others. Still, a line was forming behind her.

A moment later, she took her first cautious stride onto the ice.

"You really went during public hours?" a voice whispered in her ear.

Emma looked, startled. Hanna's face was visible for a moment before it disappeared. Emma cast it off and continued. It took a lap before it all came back to her. Suddenly, she split off from the crowd and into the center, letting herself do a figure eight. She stumbled but caught herself.

It was like she'd never stopped.

There was a clap. "Bravo!" Hanna exclaimed.

Emma looked around. Then, she saw her. Her hair in an elegant, braided updo. Her brown and silver leotard was meant to evoke Éowyn's armor.

"What?" Hanna exclaimed again. "Don't mind me. You're doing great."

Emma shook her head and joined the crowd once again, now thoroughly spooked. She caught eyes with a girl around her age. Her friend was close beside her as the girl held onto the side for her dear life.

"Just let go," Emma said.

The girl turned and looked. "I'm gonna fall."

"No, you won't," she said. "Keep yourself steady, and you'll be fine."

Once again, Emma skated away. Out of the corner of her eye, she saw the girl slowly move her hands away. She was doing it, skating.

She went back into the center, doing figure eights to clear her mind. That was what she was always best at.

"Come on, I want to see that axel," Hanna said again.

She looked at her friend, still in costume. "No."

"Why not? You act like you don't have a bronze in nationals," Hanna scoffed.

"I don't want to," Emma repeated.

"Why'd you quit?" she demanded.

"Because I wanted to be an actor instead," Emma said. "You knew that."

"You could have done both." Hanna sniffled. "You miss it though, don't you?"

"Of course I do."

"Then why do you act like it was never a part of you?"

Hanna stared grimly at her, waiting for an answer. She looked around. No one else seemed perturbed, or to even notice. "Because it hurts too much," she whispered.

Hanna rolled her eyes. "Oh, come on. Get over yourself."

"Excuse me?"

"I died thinking all of my dreams were about to come true," Hanna said. "Is there a better way to go?"

She disappeared before Emma could answer. The stream of people continued. The center of the rink was wide open for her.

If only she could remember how to do it. Of course she could. She shook her body, closed her eyes, and let herself glide. Then, she twirled up into the air.

Not just once or twice, but three times.

She landed with a beaming smile.

The girl from before was watching her with awe.

"Holy shit," she said. "You're like, a real skater."

"I used to be," Emma whispered.

SHE FOUND Jason in the atrium right after she'd changed back into her clothes. She still had an hour to kill and was figuring out what to do for dinner when he'd sat next to her, promising to bring them both Taco Bell.

"It's good to see you," he said. "Thank you so much for coming."

"Of course."

"I'm going to say a few things first, and then I'll introduce you, okay?"

Emma nodded. "Sounds good."

He'd noticed her shaking. "You're going to be great."

There were about twenty people there in all, including her parents. Emma had only taken a few bites of her burrito. She could never eat much when she was nervous. Jason had conveniently forgotten to mention that the local news would be coming, so she had to tune them out, too.

Right at the beginning of the ceremony, they'd taken off the tarp. It was a beautiful plaque. Hanna, her hands up in the air, smiling. Vanessa beside her. Their names were printed at the bottom. "HANNA LOUISE & VANESSA CAITLIN FINK. FOREVER IN OUR HEARTS."

Everything was a blur as Emma sat beside her parents in the front row, rubbing her hands together to try and stop her nerves as they listened to Jason speak.

Finally, he said, "to tell you more about my daughter, I'd like to introduce Emma Lacey. She's very generously traveled from New York City to be here." He looked at her. "Emma, come on up?"

Her parents both reassured her as she stood.

Past Jason, she saw Hanna standing, giving her a smile. "You got this!" she mouthed.

Jason placed a fatherly hand on Emma's shoulder as she approached the podium.

"Hi, I'm Emma. I used to compete alongside Hanna although she was much better than I ever was."

The crowd laughed at this. Emma bit her lip to contain a smile as she continued.

"There's a lot I could say. A lot I was thinking about saying. But I want to tell you all a story about how I became friends with Hanna Fink. We met in eighth grade when I joined this club. And we bonded over *The Lord of the Rings*. She always said that when she did make it to the Olympics she was going to make an impression on everyone by modeling her routine after her favorite character, Éowyn. Because it would be different. It would make her stand out. She never wanted to be ordinary. And I never knew why she was even friends with me."

Emma paused to wipe a tear, noticing others in the crowd were crying too.

"But I think if Hanna were here, she'd tell us not to be sad because she was happy in the end. Was her life really about what was unfulfilled or about the impact she did make in her short time? A day before she died, she texted me that she'd made Olympic Trials. And… I'm never going to forget her. I hope this plaque means no one else will, either. Thank you."

As Emma rushed away from the podium and collapsed into her seat, her mother let her fall into her arms.

. . .

THAT NIGHT, before bed, Emma was looking for something in particular. She just hoped she still had it. After twenty minutes of looking, it emerged at the bottom of a bin underneath her bed, still secured in its box. She held it gingerly in her hands.

The bronze medal.

Denver. 2015. It was the one and only time she'd placed above Hanna. When the final scores were announced that day, Hanna excitedly took her friend into her arms. "YOU'RE AMAZING!" she squealed.

Emma blinked back tears. After a momentary hesitation, she packed it in her suitcase.

fragments of another life

CAMILLA DOESN'T GET into her car that day with the intent to crash it, but the act has been a long time coming. The last straw is finding out she's lost her job, the very one she worked so hard to get after six months of living on credit cards and loans from her dad that they both knew she was never going to be able to pay back.

She can't start at square one again.

She's going to be thirty in a month, and she's tired of trying.

A day after the layoff, she drives to her old temp agency in Hollywood to see if she can get reinstated. As she rounds the bends of Barham Boulevard, she thinks to herself, *what am I doing?* How long would she sit around at the temp agency, only to not know if they could actually help her?

The cars around her woosh by. She's been behind a Bentley for the past fifteen minutes.

Must be nice. Must be really nice.

Camilla can't get a good look at the driver, but still, she can't help but wonder who they are; a producer or someone famous, maybe? Meanwhile, the check engine light on her dash seems to taunt her with its bright orange glow. It came on last week and hasn't been off since. She's hated her crappy little Mitsubishi Mirage for a while now, but it *needs* to hold on. She can't lose her car.

Spaced out, she almost rear-ends the Bentley but breaks just in time.

That's a relief. The last thing she needs is to be held liable for some rich jerk. As she takes deep, heavy breaths to try and stop her shaking body and fast-thumping heart, she glances at a nearby billboard. It's advertising some movie she hasn't heard of and isn't going to see. Of late, she can't even go to the movies. It hurts too much.

She starts to disassociate when she turns onto Cahuenga. She swerves into another lane and someone honks at her.

Camilla looks at Waze. Another twenty-five minutes to go five miles. Back home, covering the same distance would take her ten. It's one of her least favorite things about the city.

Watch her car break down before she even gets there, right in the middle of traffic.

She can't do this anymore.

Camilla saw the future ahead of her; sending countless job applications only to never hear back. She had contacted USC's career office a while back, and they'd said her resumé was perfect. Still, some student worker had redone it to optimize it for the right keywords and make it aesthetically pleasing.

It had done nothing at all.

She inches closer to Hollywood. The gaudy tourist trap that is Hollywood and Highland mocks not only her, but everyone that comes to visit.

She's done.

Already in the right lane, she hits the gas and swerves off the road. She doesn't stop until she slams into a concrete wall.

"CAMILLA," a voice calls. "Time to get up."

She opens her eyes, suddenly aware of the sound of chirping birds. A soft blanket covers her body. She opens her eyes. She's in her childhood bedroom; everything is pastel. She glances at her reflection in a nearby mirror; she has the same long chestnut hair, the same gaunt face and eyes that are too big for her head, but something's different. The pink cotton pajama pants and a white lace tank top draping her body actually make her feel pretty.

There's a knock. "Sweetie?" The door creaks open. It's her mother, Lillian. Her cheeks are rosy and full. Even the claw clip holding up her thick blonde hair can't hide how luscious it is. She hasn't looked this way in years, not since —"Are you awake?"

"Now I am," Camilla says, sitting up.

"I'm making blueberry pancakes," Lillian announces. "And scrambled eggs. Bacon, too."

Camilla manages a smile. Her mouth waters as she smells maple syrup and coffee from the next room.

Lillian comes into the room, sits on the bed and puts the back of her hand on Camilla's forehead. "You're burning up."

"What's going on? I was in my car—and you're..." Camilla can't bring herself to say the word. *Dead.*

As she starts to heave, Camilla's mother strokes her cheek. "Sweetie, what's wrong?"

"I watched you die," Camilla whispers after a beat.

Lillian just laughs. "You must have had a bad dream." She smiles, and Camilla smiles back as her stomach audibly rumbles. "Coffee's ready. Come get your cup."

She stands and follows her mother out.

The only time Camilla remembers the kitchen being this clean is when she was twelve and her mother invited a man she was seeing over to the house. It didn't work out. But now, it's perfect and clean. Other than that, it's all the same: the white cabinets, the watercolor prints, and the woodcut by the door that says "so much life in one little world" in blue cursive script. There's even a vase of lilacs on the table. She feels the spring breeze flows in through the open windows, closes her eyes and inhales it as her mother goes to the stove and turns the pancakes on the griddle. She gestures to the coffee pot. "Get it while it's hot and fresh."

Camilla breaks from her daze and opens the cupboard. Her eyes are immediately drawn to the mug from the Warner Brothers studio tour. The one that says "director."

Her hand wraps around the handle as she considers. She'd been so happy the day they'd bought that her first time in LA, when she was sixteen.

No. She's done with all of that. Her eyes drift again to the Los Angeles one, the one with 1995, the year Camilla was born, printed on it. Her mother always loved telling the story about visiting LA when she was pregnant and buying the mug because she'd "just had a feeling" there'd be a connection between the city and her daughter.

No. Camilla's done with California, too.

Like her mom said, it was all a bad dream.

She finally picks out one with a Dalmatian puppy. She takes it out and puts it beside the coffee pot, hesitating for a moment. She looks at the puppy's beady eyes, thinking instantly of *101 Dalmatians*, the first movie she ever loved.

By the time Camilla's poured her cup and taken a seat at the table, her mother's prepared her plate. Looking at it, she's suddenly ravenous. After years of subsiding on Pop-Tarts, ramen, and frozen meals, she forgot how much she missed her mother's cooking.

"*Bon apétit*," Lillian says. She takes a seat and joins Camilla.

"It feels good to be home," Camilla says.

Lillian looks confused. "What do you mean?"

"Haven't I... been away? I live in California. I have for... over ten years now." Forcing herself to vocalize the length of time makes tension creep into her neck and shoulders, as if she needed a reminder of how worthless it all had been.

Lillian gives her an empathetic look. "Sweetie, you must have *really* been out cold. You've never lived in California."

Camilla pauses. "If I say *Nighthawks*, does that mean anything to you?"

"Your movie!" her mother exclaims. "Of course! That was so nice to see it premiere at the festival, on the big screen."

"So," Camilla says, "I made that one short and...?"

"You told me you didn't want to do it anymore," Lillian says. "Remember, you used to be so into going to LA. I don't know what happened. Not that I'm complaining. It's nice having you close."

"Close?" Camilla asks.

"Sweetie," Lillian replies with a laugh. "You had too much to drink last night, so you decided to stay over."

What? "I'm sorry, I don't remember..."

"Jack was working late so you came over to try my new drink recipe."

Jack? If her mother means Jack Brewer... breaking up with him was one of the hardest things she'd ever done. Maybe they would still be together if she'd never left, but it was impossible to say. The last she'd heard of Jack was that he'd gotten married and had a kid. Her head spins as she picks at her pancakes.

"Sure," Camilla says. "Anyway, I still made my movie?" She'd come back to Springdale and made it all with a local cast and crew when she was twenty-three. Even though it had destroyed her in more ways than one—she'd taken out two loans to fund it since the Indiegogo had raised less than $500–she convinced herself it was in service of something. Interesting that it was still a part of this reality.

"You sure did," Lillian says proudly.

"What do I do for work?" Camilla asks.

"Next time, we're cutting you off earlier," Lillian says, teasing. "I would hope you're still at Channel 5. I ran into the Olsens yesterday and they're so proud of your promotion."

Camilla forces herself to smile.

Her mother gestures to the pancakes on Camilla's plate. "Come on, eat up. They're getting cold."

As the two continue to eat, Camilla looks around. She feels safe. Maybe the life she thought she lived was all in her mind and *this* is real life.

After breakfast, Camilla goes back to her room to get dressed. She notices the phone on her dresser now. It's the newest model. And the screen isn't cracked. It's pristine. She turns on her phone and it lights up with a text from Jack. The contact name has a heart beside it.

> Gm beautiful

She goes to her home page. At first, it's normal. She sees it's Saturday. 75 degrees and mostly sunny. But, other than the one text, there's nothing. Her email doesn't load. She has no saved photos. She goes to Google and types in her name.

She sees a Facebook post, announcing her promotion to Executive Producer at Springdale's Channel 5. A headshot she barely recognizes, in a blazer, white blouse, heavily made-up, her mouth in a tight line.

Before she turns her phone off, she goes back to the text, her hands shaking as she replies.

> Hi- just had breakfast and going for a walk

His reply is immediate.

> Ok 😅

After getting dressed and taking the lavender canvas purse she knows is hers from off its hook, she tells her mother she's going out.

"Where?" Lillian asks.

"For a walk," she replies.

"You're feeling better, then?"

Camilla smiles dryly. "Yes."

"Not hungover?"

"Not all all."

"It's a beautiful day for it," Lillian says. "Have fun."

CAMILLA DOES a double take when she sees the car parked in the driveway. A Bentley. It's a convertible. White, with red leather seats. She gulps, and her hand moves to her purse's front pocket. The Bentley keys are inside, and she unlocks it with a click.

She hesitates, locking it again, not ready to get behind the wheel. She needs the exercise anyways.

SPRINGDALE, Missouri, her little town thirty miles outside of St. Louis, always had an air of unreality to it. Placed right along the Mississippi River, the only thing important to say was that the town ran an hourlong steamboat cruise every day between April and September. But today, it feels especially unreal. The sun shining brightly, the green grass, the perfect sky, the chirping birds.

It's warm enough that the steamboat's probably running. She can walk there from here and check it out. She'll buy her ticket and relax with a mint julep on the deck—non-alcoholic, of course, since the place is family-friendly—while she waits to board.

She's just entering the town square and can see the sparkling river in the distance, hear the sound of the boat and the laughter of children, when she sees the poster.

It's for a movie. Coming to the single-screen Springdale Cinema. She doesn't recognize the two actors on the poster, but something about them is familiar. Almost too familiar. The way they dress, the way they pose in a grassy field at night—if she'd ever gotten to do the feature version of *Nighthawks*, this was what she always imagined the poster would be like. She looks up and sees the title, in its cursive pink font.

Nighthawks.
Are you kidding?

Someone beat her to it. Of course they did. She tells herself to get over it. It's not like she picked the most original title in the world. She takes a closer look, realizing it's advertising a special screening with the director in attendance. She cross-references the date on her phone. It's tonight.

Before she can take another step, she feels a hand on her shoulder. "Camilla!" a woman's familiar voice calls.

Camilla turns and does a double take when she sees who's standing before her.

It's Piper. But she can't—

Camilla has to take a moment to take in her friend's face, her brown eyes and brown hair with ombré blue tips. She looks good. Happy.

"Fancy running into you here," Piper chirps.

Camilla reaches forward and squeezes her tight. She has to know that this is really her, that she's alive and well.

"Well, hello," Piper remarks. When Camilla doesn't let go, she cheekily adds, "I missed you too. It's been such an agonizing... twenty-four hours."

They release from the hug and Camilla has to get another look at her, because she still can't believe it. She furiously blinks back tears.

Piper laughs nervously.

"All good?"

"Yeah," Camilla says, drying her eyes. "All good."

"Anyway, what are you doing out and about?"

"Just out for a walk. Thought I'd take a ride on the steamboat."

"Oh, fun," Piper says. "It's a perfect day for it."

Camilla feels the warmth that radiates from her friend's smile as she looks into her brown eyes. That terrible night three years ago when Camilla got the suicide note when she'd been sound asleep on the other side of the country—that all had to have been a part of the dream she just woke up from. "Do you want to come with? I was just going to get a mint julep first."

"Let's do it," Piper says, noticing that Camilla's still looking at the poster. "Oh, *Nighthawks*. You know the director's from here, right?"

"Cool," Camilla says nonchalantly.

"Yeah, she's like a big deal."

As they start to walk, Camilla still feels a magnetic pull to the poster, one she can't quite understand. There was something to it that went beyond the title and similarities in aesthetic.

They approach the town square. It's changed little since Springdale was first settled in the 19th century. This place must be what people imagined when they wrote stories about small-town Americana. The steamboat sits at the dock. She thinks about how exciting getting to go on the boat was when she was a kid. She hopes she can recapture some of it.

They cut through Gingham Park first. Calling it a park is a stretch, Camilla thinks. It's one city block of basic green space with two diagonal paths and a few benches, all centered by a white lattice gazebo.

"I selfishly have to say that I'm so glad you decided not to move," Piper says as they walk past it.

"Move where?" Camilla asks, stopping to look.

"Antarctica," Piper says sarcastically.

Camilla's face goes white as she realizes. "California? That was a pipe dream," she says, laughing it off. She's still focused on the gazebo. She would come here and read or write. She and Piper would sit and talk about whatever was on their mind.

The summer before junior year, she had taken Jack here. On those steps, he'd been her first kiss. A year later, there was her portfolio piece, the one that got her into USC. She'd made Jack and Piper star in a re-creation of the gazebo scene from *I Love Melvin*.

Piper snaps her fingers in front of Camilla's face. "Hello?"

"Sorry. Just... memories." Camilla gestures down the path ahead of them. "What's the director's name? The *Nighthawks* one? Do you know?"

"Millie, I think. Blanking on the rest."

Millie. That was—

No. It can't be.

They keep walking. By the time they're at the dock and in line to buy their tickets to the boat, a young man in a dark outfit taps her on the shoulder. "Camilla Winston-Brown?" he says.

Camilla nods.

The man hands her a card. "Please arrive at this address at six p.m. tonight. Don't be late."

Camilla looks. "Millie," it reads. There's an address downtown. As soon as she looks up, the man is gone. She and Piper exchange a look, and Camilla shows her the card.

"Oh my God, girl," Piper says. "Look at this. The Argyle Hotel?"

"Sure, that doesn't mean anything."

"If I were an Oscar-winning director, that's where I'd stay," Piper says.

"I'll worry about it later," is all Camilla says. She puts the card in her purse as the two approach the ticket booth.

"You're buying, right?" Piper winks at her.

"I guess," she says. She opens her purse and takes out the faux crocodile skin wallet, filled with different credit cards. She picks a random one, thick and jet-black, and pays. As Piper just smiles, Camilla wonders what her credit limit on this one is.

By the time they're on the boat, Camilla's more or less up to speed on everything. Piper's still working at the art studio. Still living with Lucas. They're planning a trip to Hawaii in the fall.

"I'm glad things are going well," Camilla says once they take a seat on the boat deck.

"Well, what about you?" Piper playfully teases. "How are you and Jack doing?"

Camilla's face goes white. "We're good."

"I'm so happy. You two are so cute together," Piper says.

All of this because she didn't go to LA. She knew what this was. The dream—it was telling her what could have happened if she'd left. It was a good thing that she didn't. She had her best friend. Her mother. A boyfriend. She'd go to... their house? She realized she didn't know where they lived. But something told her it was the mint green one on California Street. The house where Jack grew up, the one she knew he'd bought from his parents in her other life.

For the first part of the boat tour, the two friends don't say much. Camilla takes in everything she can of the rolling hills and greenery that she once called her home.

"How are you, by the way?" Camilla asks Piper. "How are you really?"

"I'm great," Piper says. "Everything's great."

"You're not… having bad thoughts, are you?"

"No, never," Piper tells her. "Camilla, I would never think that way."

The old friends exchange a look.

She remembers waking up to the text so clearly—

> I just want you to know that I'm grateful you were in my life. Please take care of yourself.

—and the sinking feeling when she called and realized it was already too late.

"You know, it's okay if you do, right?" Camilla says. "Lord knows that I—"

"Cami. Don't worry so much." Piper smiles. "Everything's okay. You're safe here."

The women part ways again at the dock. They promise to hang out again soon, but something about the interaction feels off. Everything is too perfect. But who is she to question it? Maybe this is what life is really supposed to be.

She thinks of this all as she makes her way to California Street.

Jack is on the porch with a cup of coffee. He has barely changed since high school, still with that boyish look about him. His wavy tufts of blond hair stick out to his ears. He's dressed simply, in jeans and a white henley shirt.

He sees her as she approaches. "There you are. How was your mom's?"

"It was fine," Camilla says.

He stands and greets her with a kiss. It's a quick peck, but a kiss nonetheless.

She's stunned, realizing she had completely blanked on the taste of his lips. It had been so intense at the time—the desire. There were other men that were better at kissing and at pleasuring her, but through an endless string of bad dates and timing, no one wanted her in the way she needed to be wanted. Until Jack kisses her again, she'd forgotten how much she missed the feeling.

"What's wrong, babe?" Jack says, pulling her close as he caresses her cheek.

"Nothing," Camilla whispers.

She knows what's about to happen as he leads her inside the house, into the bedroom.

She goes along with it. Might as well feel as though she's really alive.

AFTERWARD, as they lay tangled up in the white sheets, she feels absolutely certain that this all has to be a little bit real. Still, she can't help but think this room is too bare, that she would have added her own flourishes to it if she really lived here. And there's something about the way he holds her and looks into her eyes that makes her feel like she's playing a part.

"Something interesting happened in town today," she says.

"Oh?"

After a moment, Camilla gets up, putting on her shirt and fishing the card out of her pants. The one with Millie's name. She shows it to Jack.

"Oh, wow," he says, reading it.

"I don't know what she wants," Camilla replies. "I'm going to find out, leave and then... yeah."

"I need to tell you something," he says. "It's stupid."

"What is it?"

"Things are going so well with your job and I'm afraid you'll...."

"You're afraid I'll what?"

"Be too big for this town," he says. "For me."

"I'm not going anywhere," says Camilla; although, she isn't sure she believes the words that come out of her mouth. She doesn't know why. She can only clock the feeling that they ring hollow.

She lets his words sink in. She finishes getting dressed. She wants to see her mother again. "I have to go," she tells him. "I'll see you."

"What do you mean?" he says, confused.

"My car's back at the house anyways, so."

They kiss. She lets it linger before she forces herself to

pull away and leave. The sinking feeling is worse as she walks back.

It's all too perfect.

BACK AT HOME, she's met with the smell of something baking wafting from the kitchen. "Mom?" she calls.

Her mother emerges a moment later, carrying a beater. "Oh, hi sweetie!" she says. "I'm making cookies. You want a beater?"

She hands it to Camilla before she can answer. Still, she's not turning down a chance to eat a bit of homemade cookie dough. She hands it back to her mother and hugs her tightly.

Lillian laughs nervously. "Uh-oh. What do you want?"

"Nothing. Just to tell you that I love you," Camilla says, stifling tears. "I'm sorry I never said it enough."

Her mother seems confused. "How was your walk?"

"It was good," Camilla says.

"Did you forget something or are you sticking around?"

"Sticking around," she says. "Jack has to work, and I left my car so I might as well spend time with you."

Lillian smiles. "Okay."

"I'm going to lay down," Camilla says.

She spends the next thirty minutes staring at her ceiling, failing to quell the thoughts that circle through her mind.

Am I dead?

The afterlife was real all along, and I'm in it.

It's not so bad, is it? Just accept the fact that things can go right for once.

Her mom knocks.

"Come in," Camilla says, her voice creaky.

"They're ready! Get them while they're hot and fresh," Lillian says.

She obliges.

The cookies, like everything her mother makes, are perfect. The two smile as they eat them, and Lillian asks if she wants dinner.

"If you're staying, I was thinking I could make the jalapeño pasta," she says. "I haven't made that for you in a while."

"I'd love that, but…"

"But what?"

"I have somewhere to be by six," she says.

"Oh?" Lillian says curiously.

"A meeting with that filmmaker that's in town."

"Very nice," Lillian says. "We'll have plenty of time."

They don't say much as they eat.

Before she goes, she remembers the old advice to dress as the person you imagine yourself to be. She finds an ivory blouse and jeans that seem to do.

Camilla hesitates in leaving the house. There's a lot, in her other life, that she never got to say to her mother. She hugs her and says "I love you" one more time.

THE BENTLEY FEELS like it was made just for her. She savors everything about it for the short drive. Even after she pulls into a parking spot outside the hotel, she lingers for a second longer, checking her phone again. It's 5:59. She sees another text from Jack.

> Gl w ur meeting babe know ur going to be great

She sighs, shuts off her phone, and forces herself to get out of the car.

Camilla isn't sure if she's ever been inside the Argyle Hotel, but it's about one of the nicest places she's ever been. The ornate blue, the cherry-wood walls; it's hard to imagine that Springdale could even host such a beautiful place.

She's about to go to the front desk and explain when she sees the man from before. "Ms. Winston-Brown," he says. "You made it. I'll take you to Millie now."

As they ride up to the twelfth floor in the equally ornate elevator, only one question escapes her lips. "What is this all about?"

"Millie will explain," he says.

They get up to the hotel hall, to Room 1201. He knocks. Someone opens it. As he converses with a woman with an eerily familiar voice, Camilla takes a step back, hiding.

"Yeah?"

"She's here," he says.

"Let her in," the woman replies. "Thank you, Henry."

"I'm going to grab dinner," he says. "You want anything?"

"No, I'm good."

As Henry disappears back into the elevator, Millie steps out into the hall. "Camilla," she says.

Camilla turns in the direction of the voice and gets a good look at Millie for the first time. She's dressed in a gray shirt and black parachute pants. Her chestnut hair is cut in a blunt line at her collarbone, and her flip-flops show off her perfect red nails. Even with a bare face, she exudes confidence. That's to say nothing of the diamond ring on her finger.

It's like looking in a mirror.

This can't be—

It is.

"I was wondering if you'd show up," Millie says quietly. "Come on in."

The suite is decorated in the same shades of blue and gold as the rest of the hotel.

"This is nice," Camilla says.

"It's a nice hotel," Millie replies.

"Kind of a misnomer, though," Camilla says. "There's not one argyle pattern on site."

"I was just thinking the same thing," Millie says with a laugh. She gestures towards the couch. An open laptop creates a small blue glow. "Let me move this…"

She closes it and puts it on the coffee table. The two sit.

"I heard you have an Oscar," Camilla says.

Millie shrugs. "It's just a statue. Of course, it meant the world at the time, but…we woke up the next day, the same person with the same problems."

Camilla scoffs. "Not quite the same."

Millie raises an eyebrow.

"But I don't understand what's happening to me," Camilla whispers.

Millie sighs deeply. "We need to talk. First, what are you drinking? Still White Girl Rosé?"

Camilla nods.

"Coming right up," she says, walking over to the fridge and pouring two glasses. "I picked up a bottle from the store for old time's sake. I guess I've been thinking about you ever since. So, I guess this is all my doing."

"When did you start going by Millie again?" Camilla asks.

"When I decided I don't hate the nickname," Millie says. "But I'm still Camilla Winston-Brown."

Hearing her say the full name makes Camilla's surroundings blur. This beautiful, confident woman can't be her or any version of her. As much as seeing her is like looking in a mirror, it's even more like staring at a complete stranger.

Millie returns to the couch and gives Camilla her glass and keeps the other for herself.

She's distracted by the view of the town now.

Millie takes a long drink of wine and sighs. "You look awful, you know that?"

Camilla shrugs. "What do you want me to say? What's the deal with Piper, Jack, Mom?"

"I know it's what you think you want. I know you're thinking you could have had all of that if you never left."

"I've thought about it every day."

"But I also know you well enough to know that you want to go back to your life," Millie says.

Camilla says nothing.

"Am I wrong?"

"No, you're not," Camilla replies.

Millie takes a long drink. "I know you're not going to believe me, but you just have to hold on a little longer, okay?"

Camilla drinks too, now, cautiously. "If I'm really you and you're really me... there's so many questions I have. What did I—*we*, whatever—win an Oscar for?"

"I can't say," Millie replies.

Camilla shifts her gaze to the laptop. "Are you working on anything?"

"Emails, mostly. But I am writing about you."

"Oh?"

"Trying to get everything figured out with this screening tonight because people are incapable of reading emails. Ivy was sick for like two weeks and out of school so I'm trying to coordinate makeup homework from all the way over here—"

"Ivy?"

"That is your favorite girl's name, isn't it?" Millie asks.

Camilla nods. It's what she'd name her daughter if she ever had one. She looks at the wedding ring, and Millie just smiles.

"Yes. That all's going to be okay, too."

Camilla thinks about how to respond. "What year is it for you?" She eventually asks. "You don't seem that much older than me."

"I can't say."

"You can't say, or you don't want to?" Camilla challenges.

"I don't understand how this works any more than you do," Millie replies. "But if I tell you too much it'll spoil the surprise. You just have to know that you're going to get here, and you're going to figure out how to make it happen."

"I don't believe that," Camilla says. "I can't."

Millie gives her an empathetic, sisterly look. "I just want to tell you that you have so much more life to live."

"Do I, though?" Camilla replies. "Besides, it's already too late."

Millie gestures to their opulent surroundings. "Look at all of this. *You* did this. You took all of your pain and made it mean something." She wipes a tear from her eye.

Camilla's crying too, now. "You're just a vision. One I had of how I thought my life was going to be when I was twenty-one and didn't know any better."

"That's where you're wrong," she says. She takes a last long drink, finishing her glass.

"I crashed my car, okay?"

Millie bites her lip. "Oh. That complicates things, doesn't it? Well, the fact that you're here, with me, maybe there's still a shot. I know you don't want to die."

"How?"

"Because I know you, Camilla. You're *me*," Millie says. "This life here in Springdale… none of it's real. But I am, okay?"

Camilla says nothing as she watches the wine swirl in

her glass. She thinks about shrinking and disappearing into the pink liquid, into nothingness.

"You create from your heart. I love that about you. I feel like I'm losing touch with that myself. I just want you to know that you have value, okay? You *have* a life. I wouldn't be where I am without you. This is not the end of your story." Millie sniffles. "Even when things start to happen for you—and they will—it's not going to make the depression go away. That's for sure. You just have to keep going in spite of it."

"What about this movie screening? Can't I stick around?"

"It'll be your time soon enough," Millie says.

After that, they lock eyes, but the two say nothing. They just look.

As Camilla finishes her glass of wine, the scene fades like quicksand.

SHE SEES police sirens all around her first and hears officers speaking into walkie talkies. She tries to move, but moans in pain a second later, reverting back to her original seat. Her car's upright, still, but she doesn't need to see much to know the damage is bad. Everything is crumpled thin.

"We have a female driver. She's moving..." The officer opens the car door.

"Ma'am? Can you hear me?"

It takes all of her strength to nod.

He turns back to his walkie talkie. "The driver is alive. Responsive. Stand by."

"Are you hurt?"

"I don't know," Camilla croaks.

What did she do?

He leans forward, and the two lock eyes. "We're going to get you help."

She manages a weak nod.

"Everything's going to be okay."

our lifelong dreams

SHE DOESN'T REMEMBER anything before the bright light. Fluttering her eyelids open, she inhales the scent of lavender and sage and feels the silk nightgown caress her skin.

This place is familiar to her; although, she can't tell why. All that she knows is that something is waiting for her. Something she has to get to. The comforting sound of ocean waves washing against the shore dances in her ear as she sits up, taking in her room's surroundings.

The walls are white. The carpet is a mix of soft pink and blue. A reed diffuser sits on top of the mid-century modern dresser facing her, the source of the inviting floral scent.

"Welcome," a woman's soothing voice calls over an intercom. "Your journey must now begin. Your train departs from Platform A at six o'clock. Late arrivals will not be accommodated."

"Wait," she croaks, her voice dry. "What train? Where?"

She's met with silence.

She runs her fingers through her ratty auburn hair and tussles her bangs into an acceptable position, until, out of the corner of her eye, she sees a ticket.

The vintage font and brown paper makes it seem a hundred years old.

She inspects it closely.

RAILWAY TICKET

VALID THIS DAY ONLY
DEPARTS 6:00 PM SHARP!
PLATFORM A

Of course. The train. The one she has to get to. A clock sits beside her vanity. It's just before four. That gives her almost two hours. Platform A can't be that far away, so she has plenty of time.

She stands up. The dresser drawers are filled with clothes. They're all so perfect it's hard for her to pick an outfit. She finally decides on a white dress with sheer lace sleeves and inspects one of the tags before putting it on. "Christine," it says in tiny script. She knows it's the name of the company, but also a name. She has a name, too.

What was it, again?

Shoes are in the bottom drawer. She slides into a pair of strapped leather sandals that felt like they were always meant to belong on her feet. A brown leather suitcase sits at its side.

She knows that she doesn't want to leave. She's only just gotten here. And she still can't quite remember anything about who she was before. She takes the ticket gingerly in her hands.

There's a knock.

She freezes. She wasn't expecting company.

They knock again.

"Come in," she says, her tone cautious.

The man who opens the door has a scruffy blond shag haircut and is dressed in royal blue. His pants are bell bottoms and his shirt is stitched with paisley. He smiles at her, warm, friendly. "Hello."

"Hello," she echoes.

"I suppose you're getting ready for your train," he says.

"Yes."

"I missed mine," he says solemnly. "So, ever since, I've been here."

She realizes her dress has a pocket, folds the ticket up, and puts it in as she faces the man. He's staring at her. No, not staring. Regarding her as if she was the most beautiful thing in the world. She raises her eyebrow.

"Sorry, it's just... you remind me so much of someone I used to know," he mutters.

"Oh," she replies. "I don't remember my name. Maybe you can help me."

"I'm Bennett. She was Vicky."

"No... it's something different," she whispers.

"Well," Bennett says. "I can help you find your way to the train, if you want."

"Would you? I just need to find Platform A by six o'clock."

Bennett smiles. "I can help with that."

She takes the suitcase in her hand, and one last look at the room. She's just become acquainted with it, and now she has to leave.

Bennett recognizes her look. "Don't worry. We all felt the same at first."

THE TWO ENTER a long hallway with plain, off-white walls. It's carpeted with slate gray shag. High windows reveal a perfect, cloudy day. She stills smells lavender and sage, hears ocean waves and chirping birds.

They walk for a while before she asks Bennett, "how are you sure this is where the train is? If you didn't make it?"

"Trust me," Bennett says.

So, she does, staying quiet until they pass a giant poster. "ROUND TABLE, LIVE IN CONCERT" it reads. She recognizes herself in the center, in sheer black, staring down the camera. On her left, slightly behind her, is a woman with long, dark brown hair, wearing a gray floral dress. Her gaze evokes curiosity and wonder. On her right is a man in a long sleeve navy shirt with a thick white stripe around the chest. His dark mop-top ends just above his brow. He smiles slyly. Looking at him stirs something in her. Familiarity. Comfort. Desire. It warms her face and makes her body tingle.

Beside it is a framed news article. "WHAT'S ROUND TABLE'S NEXT MOVE?" The headline asks. Her heart races.

She steps a little closer to read it.

Allison Carmichael, the lead singer, said the following on her band's recent success as opening act for the punk band Netherworld. "The fans are just the best. Thank you from the bottom of our hearts for coming out to the shows and for letting us share our music with you." On the recently announced deal with Pegasus Records to produce their first album, she added, "It'll be rad!" Guitarist Felix Porter said, "We can't say too much about it yet. We can't wait for you to see what we're cooking up." Drummer Christine Johnson simply stated, "Stay tuned."

That was my name, she thinks, freezing in her tracks. *Allison.*

Bennett watches her with a wry look. "Remembering?"

"You could say that," Allison mutters. Flashes of her bandmates, her closest friends, linger through her mind. "I was famous. Or, I was going to be."

"Me too," Bennett says. "Me and Vicky both."

"Until you ended up here?"

He nods.

"Why *are* we here?"

"That, you'll find out on the train," Bennett says.

Allison gestures towards her bandmates. "Am I going to them?"

Bennett shakes his head.

"Then what am I going towards?"

"You'll find out soon enough," Bennett says. The hallway takes a sharp bend rightwards, and he turns back to where they came from.

"Wait a minute, wait!" Allison cries. "I don't know where I am."

In another moment, he's out of earshot, out of sight, and she's alone.

She takes a moment to process her solitude and tries to remember.

CHRISTINE.

Felix.

There were a lot of hours, from the time she was very young, spent in Felix's basement.

She remembers his face. Them sitting on the couch. His lips soft against hers. Her first kiss. They were both fourteen.

"Alli, you know that I don't actually like you that way?" he said to her a day later.

"Neither do I," Allison whispered, trying to pull all of her strength to mask the lie.

He must have bought it.

Christine came to town that year. She and Allison were best friends first. They bonded over music first. When she introduced her to Felix, it was love at first sight. There was no stopping it. It was like all the magnetic forces in the universe pulled the two of them together, and all Allison could do was watch from the sidelines.

She pauses and remembers she's still in the hallway.

As she puts one foot in front of the other, the sound of ocean waves only grows louder.

She's headed to a door, propped open with a yellow "CAUTION: WET FLOOR" sign. Above it, there's a wooden one—"TO TRAINS"—and an arrow pointing forward.

ALLISON IS MET WITH FRESH, salty ocean air.

She's on a boardwalk lined with stands for cotton candy, ice cream, corn dogs; all of her favorite foods.

This is her home. Not Venice Beach in Los Angeles, where Round Table would eventually settle, but Hollywood, Florida. The place where she grew up. Beyond is bright green grass. Blue sky. Palm trees.

Allison looks around. This isn't the station. But there's nowhere else to go.

She turns and tries the door. Locked.

Her heart races, but a moment later, she calms herself.

The sign said this was the way. So she has to figure it out.

In the far distance is a roller coaster. She watches as a cart snakes up, down and loops in a circle. There's nothing she'd love more than a ride. She hesitates, knowing she's still carrying her bag, and that she's on a deadline.

Eventually, she finds her way to a bench, watching the cars move effortlessly along the coaster's track as she sits and releases the suitcase from her grasp. As much as she always liked the look of the old leather ones, wheels were a practical invention.

"You have time," a woman's smooth voice calls.

Allison turns toward the source. Her hands are caked

with chalk. She holds a piece in one. Between her ankle-length white dress and teased blonde hair with bangs that fall in a blunt line past her eyebrows, she looks ethereal. She sits and sets her chalk aside. Her face is young, but aged by weariness.

The woman's path is draped in an abstract, multicolored whirlwind in the sidewalk behind her. It's reminiscent of Van Gogh, Cezanne, all of Allison's favorite artists. It snakes on for blocks.

———

SHE AND FELIX went to the MoMA on tour. He'd insisted that she had to go and see the original. Christine had opted not to come. Allison had been skeptical, but it had been a surreal, almost religious experience to see *The Starry Night* with her own eyes.

"Need a minute?" Felix said with a smile as he stood beside her in the simple, white-walled room.

"I just might."

They locked eyes, causing a rush of longing to flood through her.

More happened that night. She knows it. But her brain holds her from it for now.

THE WOMAN NOTICES HER LOOKING.

"Like them?" the woman asks.

"Yes," Allison says. "I do. Did you—"

"Every stroke. I wanted to be a painter," she says. "But my husband was an actor, so I became one too."

Allison pauses, looking at the woman's sad, tired eyes. "What's your name?"

"Victoria," she says. "Everyone called me Vicky."

"Called?"

"Poor girl," Vicky whispers to no one in particular. "She hasn't figured it out."

"I haven't figured out what?"

"I suppose you're trying to catch a train," Vicky says with a scoff.

"As a matter of fact, yes." When she says nothing in response, Allison adds, "is your husband named Bennett, by chance?"

Vicky casts her gaze downward. "Yes. And you're Allison Carmichael."

"How do you know that?"

"I think I pay close attention to who copies my style."

"You're Victoria Shears," Allison says, suddenly remembering. "Your husband is…"

"Bennett Klein?" Vicky says dryly. "That's right."

Allison gulps. She'd been fifteen when she first saw *No Name*, the 1966 arthouse film. She'd instantly been enamored of Victoria Shears and of Bennett Klein, her paramour onscreen and off. Sitting alone in her basement on a late Friday night, surrounded by wood-paneled walls, Allison kept the volume low. It had been a recommendation, one she was told her mother couldn't know about, in case she got the wrong idea.

Suddenly, a flash of Vicky, her body caked with blood,

a bullet hole right through her temple, appears to Allison, fading again to normalcy a second later.

It takes a moment for Allison to catch her breath.

"That's alright," Vicky says. "I'm sure you saw the pictures like everyone else. Murder-suicide in the Hollywood Hills. 1968?"

Allison nods. The world around her fragments like television static as she watches Vicky's life unfold before her.

Bennett had been the child star. Vicky was a dog groomer in Delaware and a nude model on the side when they met in 1962. Her resumé was three films long, two with Bennett, and one without. The year she died, she'd been Juliet in a well-reviewed Off-Broadway production of the classic play that only lingered in grainy photographs and fading memories. It was that scarcity that drew Allison to her. Hers was a life unfinished.

The couple was glamorous but codependent. Vicky, who'd left everyone and everything she'd ever known and traveled across the country to be with her husband, got lonely and jealous. She fell heavily into substance use. Bennett was no angel; he had a temper. He cheated and got violent. One night, Vicky, the beautiful, budding actress, snapped. She killed her husband while he was sleeping before turning the gun on herself.

"It's not true, right?" Allison finally says.

"Of course it's true," Vicky whispers. "But you had to have known that, right? It's what gave you... allure? Taking after me?"

"No," Allison says defensively. "You had to have a reason for what you did."

"I wanted him to die," Vicky says. "I think I would have turned out alright if he and I had never met. But we did. I'm at peace here, and he is too."

The silence lingers.

It takes Vicky's hand on Allison's shoulder to steady her. "Don't be afraid."

"But you were—" *So young.* The words don't quite escape her tongue.

"Twenty-seven. We both were," Vicky says. She gestures back at the roller coaster. "I know you want to ride it."

Allison leaves her suitcase at the bench. Vicky promises it'll be safe.

As they walk to the coaster, Allison, watching the sunlight glitter off of Vicky's dress, finds herself with so many questions.

"Did he—" Allison starts.

"Deserve it?" Vicky says with a scoff. "Depends on your point of view. Like I said, if we'd never met, I think it would have been alright."

Allison thinks of Bennett, forever wandering the halls where she arrived. The two of them, separated by a barrier, just out of reach, stuck in this space. Wherever she's going, wherever the train is taking her, she has to be sure to get there.

They're at the roller coaster now. It's Old West themed. Just like the movies she used to watch on TV with Mom and Dad. The three of them used to come to a place like this when she was young, before the divorce, before Dad moved to Austin, married Stacy, and had a family of his own. A family he'd done right.

There's no line. Only a painted cartoon horse telling her how tall she has to be to ride. Allison turns back to Vicky. "You're coming, right?"

Vicky takes a deep breath. "Sure, I suppose."

"What's wrong?"

"Bennett asked me to marry him on top of a Ferris wheel in Paris," she says, her tone melancholic. The anecdote is familiar. Allison remembers the black and white photo from that 1964 Paris trip, and how Vicky Shears was everything she wanted to be.

They get into the car.

For a moment, as they fly through the air, she's pure adrenaline.

Nothing else matters.

WHEN THEY GET BACK to the bench, Vicky tells Allison that she can't go any further.

Allison lingers. "What's waiting for me on the train, Vicky?"

"How would I know?" she says nonchalantly.

"I ran into Bennett when I first woke up here," Allison finally says.

"He missed his train," she replies.

"And what about you?"

"I chose to stay," Vicky says. "But just so you know, once you decide, you can never take it back."

"What if I don't make it in time?" Allison says. "I have no idea where I'm going."

Vicky points down a pathway of chalk art, towards the road.

Allison looks towards the peaceful street and the palm-lined storefronts without a car in sight, breathing heavily. A large, ornate clock that towers amongst the buildings beats with the announcement that it's five.

Did all of that really take an hour? It must have.

There is so much more she wants to say—not just to her, but to Bennett too—but she knows she needs to keep going.

Allison lingers, gripping her suitcase tightly as she continues down the path.

SHE REMEMBERS WALKING through these streets, singing to herself on her walk home from school, blasting favorites on her Discman. "Mr. Blue Sky" was a favorite. She'd been a sophomore in the fall of 1996 when her vocal trill at the end of the chorus had caught the attention of a middle-aged passerby.

He'd smiled at her. "You have a lovely voice."

It had taken Allison a moment to realize someone was talking to her. "Thank you."

"Are you a singer?"

"I don't know," Allison said with a nervous laugh. "My friend plays guitar. So he gives me a lot of music." Forcing herself to call Felix a friend and not what she really wanted was enough to evoke a lump in her throat.

"I run a music school downtown," the man said, introducing himself as Fred Chesney. "Think about it."

He became her vocal coach. He told her she had what it took to be famous and encouraged her to ditch the striped shirts, overalls and converse for a more feminine, grown up look. Something timeless, ethereal. He told her to watch *No Name* that year. She started doing her eyeliner thick, curling her hair, and wearing pastel dresses, the fashion always out of time.

Christine took an immediate dislike to Fred. "There's something off about him," she said.

"What do you care?" Allison replied. "Jealous?"

Christine scoffed. "Alli, he's older than your dad!"

"So?"

Allison knew Fred's interest in her was more than professional. She'd never had any intentions of ever reciprocating it, not really. But it was after that, after a lesson one day, that she let him feel her up.

It wasn't the only time, nor was it the furthest they'd gone. Allison never really liked it, but she convinced herself it was better than having no one and nothing. It was always in Studio 1, after their lessons, and done in a few minutes.

It went on for a few months before Christine told her that she and Felix were going to start a band. There was no one they'd want as their lead singer other than her. She practically strong-armed Allison into it.

It was near the end of sophomore year when she called

Fred's music school, pretending to be Allison, and said that she was canceling all of her scheduled lessons and un-enrolling because she was moving out of state.

Allison had no idea until she showed up to a lesson one afternoon to a very confused front desk, who informed her that the cancellations had already been processed, and that Mr. Chesney's schedule was booked out for the next three months.

The next day, at school, she confronted Christine and Felix.

To Christine, she said, "What did you do?"

To Felix, "Did you know about this?"

"You deserve so much more than that fucking creep," Christine said.

"Look," Felix told her, "we really think this band could be something. But we can't do it without you."

That summer, Round Table came to be in the trio's alternating basements.

In the fall, Fred's daughter accused him of sexual assault, leading to a messy court case.

Through endless probing, Allison swore to everyone that nothing had ever happened between her and Fred.

There was one accuser. Another student, not unlike her. The disappointment on her tear-stained face as Allison insisted over and over that she couldn't help would always stay with her.

She didn't want to be a victim. She wanted to live her life.

Her bandmates were the only ones that ever knew the truth, the only ones that understood.

Because of that, their bond became unbreakable.

BACK TO THE EMPTY STREET.

At the end of the block, she tires of carrying the suitcase. Something tells her she doesn't need it, so she leaves it on a bench.

A weight leaves her shoulders as she looks around. The sun is quickly sinking in the sky, and she still has no idea where she's going.

She walks a few paces before the faint sound of festival music catches her attention. Where is it coming from?

"Vicky? Bennett?" Allison cries, even though she knows it's hopeless.

The source is under a cast iron archway, connecting two buildings, and a yellow brick path. As she gets closer, a sugary, buttery smell grows more potent and inviting.

She sees him sitting on a bench.

She barely recognizes him sans makeup and dressed in a simple black t-shirt and jeans. But she knows it's him from the way he calls her name.

"Allison," Mason Grant says. "Come sit." The lead singer of Netherworld—the original one, who Round Table never met—has two paper plates with fried elephant ears beside him.

She does. "It's just like—"

"The county fair?" Mason says with a warm smile. "When you were growing up?"

Allison nods emphatically.

It isn't until Mason offers her a plate that she realizes

how hungry she is. She immediately scarfs hers down. He delicately picks at his.

"Don't tell me you missed the train too," Allison mutters.

"No, I'm here to help you," Mason says.

"With what?"

"Passing on," Mason says calmly. "It's nothing to be afraid of."

Allison takes another bite of her elephant ear and processes. "So, I'm dying? Or I'm already dead? Can't I go back?"

Mason shakes his head.

"I just woke up here," Allison whispers. "I can't be…"

———

SHE REMEMBERS SO MUCH ALL AT ONCE.

The concerts that started off small and got bigger once they packed everything into a van and headed west.

In LA, the interviews on talk radio that called her a millennial Vicky Shears. The black and white modeling, too. One of the photographers was David.

He wanted sex and to share his drug habit.

She was in love, so she went along with whatever he wanted.

For a while, she was finally over Christine and Felix. It was exciting to get to play in the band with them and actually enjoy it without any complicated feelings getting in the way.

She found out David, the photographer, had been seeing someone else—someone he'd just asked to marry him—right as they were about to leave with Netherworld on tour.

Her name was Brenda or something square like that. She was a grocery store clerk. Quiet. Demure. She'd make a perfect housewife.

Somehow, it all led to a rainy night in LA.

MASON'S LOOK brings Allison back.

"What happened to me?" is all she can say.

"Do you want to know?"

"It depends," Allison says, her voice shaky. "What's waiting for me on the train?"

"That's the thing," he replies, his voice even. "None of us can know."

"But what if I want another shot? I want to go back to my life."

"Allison," Mason says. "There's something I think you should see."

Behind them, an old TV on a wooden cart appears. Mason turns it on. Suddenly,

she sees—

—Herself, in a hotel room, her eyes red, her makeup smudged. It's a hopelessly black night as rain smears down the windows. Allison, alone, pops barbiturates into her mouth. Next, she alternates between screaming into a pillow and taking swigs of whiskey, straight from the bottle.

IT ALL COMES BACK to her now.

Allison was newly single when they left on tour. She knew Christine and Felix were fighting a lot, but still, she did her best to keep to herself.

It lasted until Toronto, when they met the band. There, Payton Erhle, the guitarist, assumed that Felix and Allison were the couple. At a party, he told Allison that it was obvious to him how Felix felt.

"Trust me," he said. "I know it's tricky because of the band and all, but I know what I see."

As they followed Netherworld from city to city all over the world through a stream of concerts and parties, Round Table's buzz grew. Throughout it all, Allison continued to notice the fights. They were gasoline on the fire of her heart, which only became more and more difficult to ignore.

In New York, the trio got a call to see a manager. It was there that Christine and Felix booked their first separate hotel room.

Van Gogh. The MoMA. It was that March.

Back at the hotel, Allison and Felix both started drinking. One thing led to another—

Allison closes her eyes. She can't think of it anymore.

SUDDENLY, she's in the alleyway with Mason again.

"Christine found out by the time we got back to LA," Allison says, her breathing heavy. "Now I remember.

That's right, it was June. My birthday was in July. I was going to be twenty-five."

"You were going to leave the band?" Mason prompts.

"I told Felix that being a quarter of a century old meant I was going to have to rethink my life." Allison blinks back tears. "I think I would have, even if she hadn't… I was tired of embarrassing myself. Tired of following him around everywhere because I thought one day he'd love me too." She can't stop herself from crying now. "We never even got to record the album."

Suddenly, the image on the TV screen shifts to another pitch-black night. Felix sits alone in a hospital room, his expression vacant. His body is there but his mind isn't. Outside, a fervent downpour rages. As thunder rumbles, a lighting strike, not unlike a concert strobe, brightens the dim space. Allison can only just barely make out her shadowy, limp figure lying on the bed. "Wait, am I still—"

"Just barely," Mason says.

"So, if I make it, then I can go back, right?" Allison replies, lighting up.

"That's not up to us, unfortunately."

"I…" Allison's voice is weak.

"What is it?" Mason says.

"I don't want to go. That night… it was going to be a new beginning for me."

"But you mixed dangerous drugs," Mason says.

"Like we didn't do that every night on tour!"

"You did," Mason reminds her. "I never met you." As he speaks, the bruise around his neck, left from the rope he hung himself with, grows more and more visible.

"Yeah?! Why is that?" Allison demands. "You chose to—"

Mason's skin grows paler and bluer by the second. "I wanted the pain to stop."

"What are you talking about?! Everyone loved you! Your wife! Kids! Your bandmates! Why would you throw it all away?"

In response, Mason's mouth is tight, but his warm brown eyes exude a wistful longing. "The beyond isn't so bad. The key is to not be afraid."

With that, a bright light calls Allison forward.

She stands up. Facing her is a steep, inflatable yellow slide that descends into the clouds. She looks back. It's all shrouded in darkness. Everything from a moment before is gone. She hesitates.

Her wrists shake as she steadies herself down to a sit and she sticks her feet out in front of her. Then, she takes a deep breath and lets herself glide.

On the way down, she thinks of a conversation between her and Christine. Freshman year of high school. They were sitting on the beach with ice cream.

"You and Felix are just friends, right?" Christine said.

"Of course," Allison replied.

"I like him," Christine admitted, blushing. "Do you know if he's said anything about me?"

Next, she thinks of when they first heard about the Netherworld gig.

Christine's eyes were on her as Felix hugged her first.

Later, over beers, Allison made the two of them

promise that whatever happened next, they weren't going to change as people.

Her other memories are too many to count:

Riding the London Eye.

The first time she sang to 50,000 people.

Seeing camels in India and kangaroos in Australia.

Bathing in Iceland's hot springs and experiencing the Northern Lights.

The bacon cheddar croissants she'd get down the street from her place.

It was across from an animal shelter. Allison would walk through sometimes, admire all the dogs, and imagine the one she'd get once she'd set down roots.

The slide comes to an end, setting her down at a red carpeted platform.

There's another "TO TRAINS" sign, pointing right. She hears the rumble of engines.

The sound is so booming it evokes a grandness to the railroads from long before her time, one that fell away with the dawn of air travel.

Allison follows.

She walks and walks down the vaguely circular hall. Somehow, she doesn't get tired.

When she comes to a skywalk, she stops.

She's not ready, is she?

———

SHE WANTED something to happen that night.

The regrets hadn't surfaced until the next morning, when she and Felix were lying in bed.

He'd enjoyed it. She had, too. That's probably what scared them the most.

"Alli, I love Christine," he told her. "We're just going to pretend this never happened."

A week later, in Chicago, Allison got a terrible case of food poisoning. Christine came to her room with Pepto-Bismol and comforted her as she threw up in the toilet.

Later, she brought her ginger tea and sat at her bedside. All the while, Allison thought, *I don't deserve this.* Through her profuse thank yous, all Christine said was that she knew Allison would do the same for her.

How can she catch her train without any resolution?

Maybe there's still time.

She takes a deep breath and continues on.

Nothing except dusk is visible beyond the floor-to-ceiling windows at first. Then, she sees Christine, standing under dark clouds. Her hair's different. It's cut to her shoulders and she has bangs. She's alone in a cemetery. She wears a black raincoat, hood pulled high over her head, as the rain dribbles down her body.

Allison watches as Christine collapses to a kneel and starts sobbing. "You fucking bitch!" she says. "Why didn't you tell me when you had the chance?"

Allison opens her mouth to speak, but she's completely mute.

"I think I always knew," Christine says. "Well, of course I always knew. But you didn't have to fucking die."

She can only watch as Christine descends into a

sputtering mess. She wants to hug her, to apologize, to take not just that night, but all the days and nights she invited the possibility of the worst kind of betrayal.

She can't quite explain what happens next, how the clouds part and the rain stops.

But Christine seems to understand. That's all that matters as she stops crying, looks up at the sky, and manages a dry laugh.

AHEAD, out of the corner of her eye, Allison sees the classroom. The bright red, yellow and blue walls, affixed with paper stars. The low desks with green trim. The chalkboard. Allison looks at the clock in the hall opposite her.

It's 5:50 PM. She has just enough time.

She goes in and turns on the lights.

She sees her name on the desk in the middle of the leftmost row, the one closest to the windows, seeing nothing but bright light beyond.

Her drawing rests atop it. Allison has to kneel beside it to see it better. The crayon, all in blue, of a mountain, and princess standing atop it.

"Why did you only use one color?" Mrs. Quincy asked.

"Because it's monochromatic," Allison, at six years old, proudly announced.

"And what did you draw?"

"It's me," Allison said. "When I'm all grown up."

"On top of the world?"

"Yes," Allison said.

Mrs. Quincy just smiled at her.

It's 5:55 as she leaves the room, forcing herself to not look back. The engines are even louder now. Finally, a platform comes into view, and her simple carpeted surroundings give way to vintage architecture. The top of the train pokes out from here. In life, she only ever saw ones like this, with their chimneys and rounded fronts, in old illustrations and sepia-toned photographs. This one's Tiffany Blue, though, trimmed with gold. There was a camera flash—

"SHE'S AN AUBURN AUDREY HEPBURN," Felix said, snapping the picture. "Try saying that five times fast."

It was a warm day on 5th Avenue, but the trees were still bare. Allison wore big sunglasses and held a pastry bag as she posed outside of the famous store.

She took a bite of her chocolate croissant and smiled at him. "Alright, George Peppard," she said. "To the MoMA?"

ALISON SHAKES her head and wipes her damp eyes. No more memories. It's time.

There are two staircases she could take. Both go down. In gilded letters on the wall, 'A' goes left, and 'B' points right. Allison reaches into her pocket to make sure she still has her ticket.

It's there. Safe and sound.

Suddenly, she stops, her view of the black-and-white tiled floor and the carpeted steps below wobbly.

She looks back, thinking of Felix in her hospital room.

Is there a chance—?

"Excuse me, m'am," says a woman in a train uniform, ascending the opposite set of stairs. "Are you lost?"

Allison looks. It's Christine. "Just trying to find platform A."

Christine points back in the direction she's heading in. "You'll have it practically to yourself today. Follow me. I'll make sure you get comfortable."

Felix, also in uniform, takes her ticket as she enters the airy car. "No luggage today?"

"None."

"Make yourself at home," he says with the same smile that never failed to light her entire world. "It'll be a long journey, but it'll be worth it once we get there."

"And where are we going?"

"The Great Beyond," he says.

"And what can you tell me about it?"

He gives her a knowing look, an acknowledgment that he can't say, and points down the train car. "Any of the open seats, m'am."

the game of life

IMOGEN SAW HIM ON A TUESDAY, on Milwaukee's first warm summer night after everyone else had already left the bar. Technically, it was the early hours of Wednesday morning, a quarter past two. The bar would close in forty-five minutes, but it being the middle of the work week, she was expecting to have that time to herself. She'd been fantasizing about being home and getting to put her feet up. They'd been killing her all night. That was the worst part of Jim getting rid of those bump mats. The soles of her ratty Converse weren't enough.

She'd come back from cleaning the bathroom when she saw him sitting, staring out towards the door. The nightly playlist had long since abandoned The Killers and was now playing some kind of alternative rock she only half recognized.

She got a look at his face. Between his curly dark hair, light stubble on his chin, and deep brown eyes, he was cute. He wore a gray denim jacket over a black shirt and jeans. "Can I get you anything?"

"Still deciding," he said. "Give me a second."

"Sounds good," she replied. "Holler when you're ready." Finding the nearest rag, she pretended to be occupied with wiping down the counter while she dispelled the flush that was rushing through her.

Of course he wasn't the first cute customer. He wasn't even the first customer who'd come in alone without saying much, begging for someone with whom to share his life story.

No—she couldn't get involved.

She felt his eyes on her still as she moved from the counter to the glassware. This, she'd need to focus on, lest Jim yell at her again. She couldn't lose the job. If she did, she'd have nothing, and that would mean—

Imogen eyed the clock. Last call. She'd forgotten.

She got the man's attention, informing him.

"Old Fashioned," he said in a smooth voice.

"Coming right up," she replied with a smile.

His eyes stayed fixed on her as she poured the Old Fashioned's ingredients into the shaker. It was the first drink she'd ever learned how to make. Whiskey first. Then bitters, sugar, and orange. Its popularity had always befuddled her. On a given night she would make six or seven. She supposed people who passed through this bar wanted to feel more cultured than they would have downing any old PBR.

"You got a name?" Imogen finally asked him.

"Call me Luca," he said.

"I'm Imogen."

He smiled at her, and she focused in for a moment on his eyes. They were probably just dark brown, but they looked black in the bar's dim light. "What's your story, Imogen?" he asked.

As he grinned, she realized there was no denying it. He was really fucking hot. Besides, where to even begin? He'd just asked her such a loaded question. "How much time do you have?" she asked after a beat.

"All the time in the world," he replied.

Imogen took a half-step forward to get a better look as she moved the shaker back and forth. "Shaken, not stirred, Mr. Bond," she said in a British accent, shamelessly flirting.

His face was perfect.

But his eyes...

They were definitely black.

Or were they?

Luca was smirking at her. A moment later she realized why. She'd missed the glass and instead was pouring Old Fashioned right onto the counter.

"Oh, gosh," she said, setting everything aside and moving swiftly to wipe it all up. "It's that time of the night."

"Technically, it's morning," he said.

Imogen blushed as she dumped out everything that remained in the shaker. "I'm going to make things fresh for you. I'll make this right."

He didn't say anything—he just continued to stare as she remade the Old Fashioned. Whiskey first. Then, bitters, sugar, and orange. Just like she'd been taught. Just like she'd done so many times before. There was a rhythm to making drinks that Imogen had always appreciated, a routine. She'd needed it in those months when she'd first come to Jim, when she had nothing else.

"You were asking me about my life story," Imogen said, remembering his un-responded to comment that still hung in the air. "Well, I've been at this bar for... it'll be eight years this July."

Luca scoffed. "Eight years, huh?"

"It was supposed to be temporary," Imogen said quietly.

"So why wasn't it?" he asked.

Imogen took a deep breath. She needed a moment to answer that question, and she needed to focus on finishing the drink. She couldn't do both at once. A moment later, she handed Luca the Old Fashioned. Their hands brushed as she did so, and she thought that his hand seemed very cold. "It still could be, I think," she said. "I just haven't had a better opportunity."

"And yet," he said, "you once played Nina in *The Seagull*."

Imogen gulped.

She must have been frozen, because next, he probed, "at the Rep?"

That show was nine years ago. There was no way that anyone still remembered.

"How do you know that?"

"I saw it," he replied. "And I remembered thinking you were going places."

"I did, too," she whispered.

"So, what happened?" His tone was sharp and biting.

All of the sudden, Imogen was dizzy. She had to grasp the side of the counter so that she didn't collapse. "I was going through a rough patch right after *The Seagull* closed. I was going to go to Chicago and that fell through. My boyfriend left me, my car broke down and… yeah, Jim saved me from being out on the streets."

"The owner of this bar?" Luca asked.

Imogen nodded. "Yeah… he co-signed on a place as long as I came to work for him, so, there's that." She felt butterflies race in her stomach as she got even dizzier. She didn't know why she was telling Luca all of this. She needed a drink of water, otherwise she'd confess the other, unspoken end of her bargain with Jim. She reached for a glass, only for her to drop it. They both watched as it shattered in a million pieces on the floor. "I'll get it in a second," she told Luca.

Of course she'd clean it up before Jim was in. But a part of her wanted him to find it, to finally fire her and send her on her way. Anyone else would have by now, with all of the mistakes she made. Or, maybe she'd finally stand up to him and point out that this was why the bump mats were a necessary expense after all. But he knew that. Lately, she'd begun to think he'd done it on purpose to create more work for her whenever she messed up.

"Why don't you come sit with me?" Luca asked calmly. "I'm sure you're overdue for a break."

"Sure," she whispered. "Do you want to pay?"

"Okay."

She informed him of the total.

He handed her a black card. If there were any details printed on it, they were lost to her in the haze of whatever this interaction was turning out to be.

She ran the card, and a moment later, gave him a copy of the receipt to sign.

"In a minute," Luca said.

"Of course, no rush," she replied.

"Sit," he told her again.

Wordlessly, Imogen filled a cup with water and joined him, carefully tip-toeing around the glass. She took a seat beside him, looking again into his dark eyes. "I used to be so optimistic," she admitted.

"And the world got to you?"

"You could say that," Imogen said. "I don't remember a time when I didn't want to act."

"It started with when you were a Munchkin, right?" he asked.

Imogen blushed. *The Wizard of Oz*. Her first play. She'd been four years old. It had come about because she'd asked her parents how people got to be in movies.

"They have to audition," her father had told her.

"How do I audition?" Imogen asked.

Her father reluctantly agreed to help her search for notices in the area online. Looking back, Imogen thought he'd done it to humor her, not expecting to see the perfect opportunity.

Auditions were held in a local middle school. She'd remembered thinking then how grown up and how daunting it all seemed—lockers, different teachers for different subjects, no recess. One day, she'd be in middle school too.

And from that day she'd found exactly who she was supposed to be.

"Even before that, I was always playing dress-up, creating backstories for my Barbies, stuff like that," she told Luca.

"In your interview with the *Journal Sentinel*, I was really struck when you said that you wished everyone could do a play at some point in their lives," Luca said. "Just to see the value of teamwork and putting yourself in another's shoes. I think that's really beautiful."

He'd read that, too. Of course he had. "Thanks," she whispered. "I still believe it."

"I never expected to find you here," he said.

"So, have you been following me?" Imogen asked, her tone sharp.

Luca smiled from ear to ear. Of course he had a perfect smile. "In a sense," he said. "But I'm not a stalker, if that's what you're asking."

There was something about him that she couldn't quite put her finger on. She knew she shouldn't trust him, but she did anyway. She wanted him just as much as he wanted her. He was here and he was giving her his all. That was the only thing that mattered.

"I used to come to this bar when I was a kid," she said.

"With your father, right?"

"How do you know so much about me?" Imogen asked.

"I know everything about you, Imogen Carlisle," Luca said.

Her full name. It had been a while since anyone had said it all together. Jim used to tell her she'd be famous with a name like that. "Why? Because you're such a fan?" she teased with a blush.

He nodded.

"What's my middle name?" she asked.

"Anneliese," he said plainly.

He really did know everything about her.

Who was this guy?

"It's not too late for Chicago, you know," Luca said.

"Maybe it is," Imogen whispered. "I haven't acted since *The Seagull*. And besides, Jim needs me here. He's getting older."

In response, Luca handed her the drink. "Have a sip," he said. "I know you want to."

"I can't..." she trailed off. Alcohol. It was what had gotten her into trouble the first time. At first, when Jim offered her the job, she wondered how she could be around it. But he told her that if she could get through working at a bar when she was supposed to be getting sober, she could handle anything.

"Yes, you can," Luca said. "It's one sip. Come on, it's not going to hurt you."

Imogen took the glass, taking a delicate sip at first.

"You can do better than that," he said.

She took a longer sip now. The whiskey and bitters burned her throat, but then came the sweetness of the sugar and orange, and the numbing feeling that spread through her body.

"You can have the rest," he told her. "I don't need it."

She paused, looking down at the liquid.

Her father had caught her redhanded with a Fireball when she'd come home from *The Seagull*'s last show. His voice was still in her ear. "What's wrong with you? We raised you better than that."

Her mother had joined them. "We just don't know what to do with you anymore!"

She'd packed her bags that night and gone to Ted's. That had lasted for a month before he left. She would have been on the streets if not for Jim—seriously.

She chugged until the glass was gone.

Luca watched her with a smile. "You used to come here when you were a kid? Tell me more."

"Jim was Dad's best friend," she said. "He was more of a parent than my actual ones... he was the only one whoever believed in me and my dreams."

"And yet," Luca said dryly, "you're twenty-nine and going nowhere in life because of him."

Imogen felt her stomach turn. When did she last eat? It must have been that pretzel when she first got to the bar. She knew what was coming, so she excused herself.

It all came back to her as she keeled over the bathroom toilet.

She'd been six years old.

She'd come with her dad to watch the Packers game. It was fall, Imogen's favorite time of year. Jim was working the bar.

"When I first saw you, you were a little baby," he told Imogen. "Now I thought that Sleeping Beauty had just walked through this door."

Imogen blushed.

"That's her favorite Disney Princess," her dad said.

"Well," Jim replied. "I'd heard you just got a good report card." He pushed a Sprite towards her. Earlier, he'd probed that the drink was her favorite. "That's for you." To her dad, he said, "on the house."

"Can you say thank you?" her dad whispered.

"Thank you," she muttered.

She announced that she had to go to the bathroom.

Jim said he'd show her where it was. It was automatic, how she trusted him enough to take his hand.

And she trusted him when he told her he needed to stay in the bathroom with her. To make sure she flushed correctly had been his excuse.

And trusted him still when she didn't pull her pants up all the way, and he'd fixed them for her, stroking his hand over her private parts that she still didn't know how to name. After that, her father ignored her whenever she said she didn't want to go to the bar anymore.

Jim was always around, friending her on Facebook and commenting on all of her posts as soon as she had a profile and coming to her shows when her parents wouldn't. The bathroom incident was the only time she'd been—well, whatever—until she was twenty-one, when she'd come to him because she had nowhere else to go. That was why she'd gone to him for help when her world was crumbling.

She'd suppressed being molested because she had to.

Gosh, she hated that word. It made her feel like a helpless little victim when she knew she was anything but.

He was the only person she'd given her body to other than Ted.

She'd done all of it willingly, even if she knew, deep down, that she could do better than this crusty, ugly guy forty years her senior.

He was not a good person. He never had been.

She found her way to a stand, popping a piece of gum into her mouth to freshen her breath. She was going to kiss Luca on the mouth just to prove that she could. She knew Jim would see it on the security cameras. That was the point.

Except, when she got back int the bar, he was gone. There was a note on the tray with the receipt. She didn't have a chance to read it. She didn't have the time.

Jim was there, and he'd just turned on the lights.

"Hi," she whispered. "I'm just locking up."

"What's with the glass?" he asked, slurring heavily. She smelled the alcohol on his breath and body as he approached her, stroking her arms.

He was so repulsive.

How had she ever let this man inside of her?

"I dropped one," she said. She was mad at him for being here, mad at Luca for leaving, for not being around to rescue her.

"You have to not do that," he said, leaning forward to try and kiss her neck. She backed off.

"No," she said. "You're drunk."

"You're drunk too," he said.

"Yeah, I am," Imogen said matter-of-factly. "What are you going to do about it?"

He didn't respond. He just stared at her, dumbfounded. Imogen grabbed a glass, poured herself a PBR on tap, and chugged the whole thing while he watched.

"Baby, what's gotten into you?" he said.

She saw the door and tried to dart, but he stopped her.

In the struggle, her beer glass fell. Its shards joined the other one in a cascade of what looked like the Rocky Mountains remade from glass.

She'd been once, in high school, for a theater festival in Estes Park.

That place had been one of her favorite spots on earth.

She'd always wanted to go back.

Wasn't it funny? How she'd done everything right, and yet, her life had ended up like this.

Ted had always believed that humans were trapped in the Matrix. She used to think he was crazy. Now, she was starting to believe him.

Everything moved in slow motion as Jim pinned her to the counter. Somehow, she found a burst of strength to push him away. He lost his balance, stumbled, and fell back-first in the glass.

He was weak but alive as he started blankly at her.

Her first instinct was to call the cops, to tell them what had happened.

But what if he survived?

He'd make her out to be the aggressor. And he

wouldn't get rid of her. He'd use it as an excuse to keep her close. To him, this incident would be proof that she couldn't be trusted. And if she got desperate enough to go to Mom and Dad, she knew they would only take his side.

You're going nowhere because of him, Luca had told her.

She saw the large glass shard beside his head. Carefully, she picked it up.

His eyes were wide and pleading as she brought it to his chest. "Im—"

She didn't wait for him to finish before she plunged it into his body, before she watched the light leave his eyes.

This is for everything you took from me, she thought.

The fog broke as soon as he was dead.

She'd never seen a dead person before.

She always turned away at the slightest bit of gore in movies.

And yet, she'd killed him.

He was dead.

And there was no taking that back.

If all of life was a simulation, if humans were all just stuck in the Matrix, now would be the time for her to wake up.

Somehow, she stumbled over to the counter, looking at Luca's receipt, and the note he'd left underneath his signature.

MANY THANKS,
LUCIFER

i've been here before

IT HAD BEEN weeks since Sienna had spent any significant amount of time outside. There was still no end in sight to the heatwave that held Irvine in a chokehold. Her summer was quickly disappearing in its shadow. In less than a month, she'd be back in Chicago, back to college and the city she wasn't sure she liked.

Sienna fantasized about lying face down on an iceberg as she scrolled through YouTube. Nothing interested her. She checked her phone. 120 degrees. It wouldn't dip back into the double digits until late that night. Even if the air conditioning kept her cool, the outdoors was still a sauna.

She thought about texting Gabby, just to chat, but there was a nonzero chance she'd be left on read.

She stared at her message history with Josh. Their last exchange was from right before he left on the camping trip to the Adirondacks. She'd written:

> let me know how it goes!!

He'd texted back with a thumbs up.

There was a message sitting in her drafts.

> hey so I'm here for another month if u want to hang no worries if not though haha

Sienna rubbed her eyes, closing out the text history, but not deleting the message. It had been sitting there for five days, ever since she knew he'd gotten back. She hadn't sent it in the off chance he'd reach out first.

Who knew that summer could be this boring?

She was just about ready to give up when a thumbnail caught her eye on the TV.

Five Dead, Dozens More Injured: The Sokolov Park Disaster

Sokolov Park ...

Why was that name so familiar? The thumbnail was an old, saturated color photograph of a mountain-themed roller coaster.

Sienna's heart pounded just looking at the massive structure. She never understood the appeal of roller coasters. Being whipped around, spun through the air, always feeling like she was an inch from disaster—it wasn't her idea of fun.

It was something Josh had teased her about on their junior year trip to Knott's Berry Farm. That day, there was a lot of standing on the sidelines with cotton candy and soda while everyone else lined up to ride.

Still, something compelled her to click on the video, even if doing so made her stomach turn so tightly she could barely breathe.

It began with a vintage commercial. Technicolor shots of a dance hall, go-karts, a Swan Lake-esque waterfront with picnic benches, and of course, rides all showcased Sokolov Park's grandeur. It seems it wasn't just the name that stirred Sienna with a sense of familiarity.

Sienna paused the video, realizing that she was shaking profusely. *Calm down,* she thought. *It's just a video.* Why was her body acting as if there was an intruder in the house?

Her eyes drifted to the video description as she took slow, deep breaths.

> With the recently announced reopening of the infamous Sokolov Park, I thought it would be interesting to look back at its history and the series of events that led to the derailment of its flagship coaster, killing 5 and injuring 28 on August 12th, 1967.

She resumed the video. It cut to the essayist, who explained Dmitri Sokolov's background. He was a wealthy immigrant from the Soviet Union and a brilliant engineer. Spending his life hopping around before settling in Newport Beach, Sokolov wanted to create a place that reminded him of the home he'd been forced to leave. Everyone told him it was impossible— no one wanted to go to a Russian-themed place at the height of the Red Scare. No one would even let him build it. The essayist quoted Sokolov's response to his naysayers:

> *I am an engineer, but I am also an artist. And all artists pull from their life experiences. This is mine. If I can create a place where everyone of all ages can have fun together, then we will build bridges.*

And it did. From the moment Sokolov Park opened its doors in 1951 in Chino Hills, it was extremely popular. Or it was until August 12th, 1967.

Sienna paused the video again. *That's* what it was. Her family lived a spitting distance away from the park. She must have gone when she was young and had a bad experience or something.

Wait—now she remembered. She'd had too much junk food on a trip there as a kid and had thrown up after riding one of the coasters.

That had to be it.

Sienna's phone dinged. It was Gabby.

> r u busy?

Sienna sighed and responded.

> no

Gabby's response came back a moment later.

> wanna hang at my place? Parents are gone for the weekend and the new guy at the liquor store doesnt card

Sienna would have to take an ice bath of a shower in order to prepare herself to go outside, and she was just getting into the video, but she could finish it later. She dragged herself off the couch and started to get ready.

A YEAR at UCLA had made Gabby a convert to New Age philosophy—evident from her purple bohemian dress, incense, and crystal-laden candles on her dresser. After they came back with beers and moved to her room, she wanted them to try out a past-life meditation.

"What?" Sienna said in disbelief.

"I mean," Gabby said. "It's cool to see what you visualize. The last time I did it I was a man in Ancient China that made gunpowder. You know, they say if you're drawn to the past it's because you have unfinished business in your last life."

"Was that a jab?" Sienna asked with a scoff. There was never anything she'd wanted to study *but* natural history.

"No," Gabby whispered. "I'm just saying. I think it's interesting. I go to this meditation group every week at this Buddhist temple, and yoga every other week, and we go to this tearoom after—"

Sienna raised her eyebrow. "I think LA made you a cultist."

"No," Gabby said. She laughed wryly. "You'll appreciate this."

So, Sienna agreed. She *was* curious about what she'd see, even if it was all made up in her head.

Gabby laid out blankets and pillows for the two of them. She lit the crystal candle, explaining that the clear quartz would cleanse their energy and give them clarity, and dimmed the lights.

As soothing instrumental music and a calming woman's voice relaxed them both, Sienna soon began to forget. About the heat, about her boring life, about her non-relationship with Josh and the fact that her best friend had changed in the year they'd been away at school.

Soon she was traversing a celestial pathway, barefoot, through the stars. Ahead of her was a door. She was completely and totally relaxed by the time she was guided through it.

Remember, take things as they come, the voice called. *You are always safe and protected. Now—open the door, and step into your past life.*

She did.

THE BRASS WAS cold against her hand, but everything else was warm, bright, and sunny. She thought she heard The Beach Boys on the radio coming from within. Her surroundings were hazy at first until the guide spoke again.

Look down. What surrounds you?

Yellow linoleum of a kitchen floor, cool against her bare feet. Red painted toes. A red blouse, tucked into high-waisted white shorts.

What do you look like?

She caught her reflection in the window. Her hair was shorter, a lighter shade of blonde and tied back in a mid-length ponytail. But other than that, her face was the same. She felt more confident in her own skin—lighter, more free.

Is there anyone with you?

Josh smiled as he got two Cherry Cokes out of the fridge. She was sure it was Josh. He had the same lanky frame and mop of brown hair, the same beautiful blue eyes, freckles . . .

Except here, his name was Luke. And hers—

Marilou.

What year is it?

1967.

The guide stepped back then, giving her the opportunity to explore this life.

———

HE TASTED LIKE CHERRY COKE. The tingle of his lips on hers was so vivid that it stirred something in Sienna. This was certainly a type of kiss she didn't know in this life.

They were in his house, she knew. His kitchen. He pulled away and smiled as he put his hands on her shoulders. He gazed deeply at her.

"What?" she—no, Marilou—said with a giggle.

"Just taking you in," Josh—no, Luke—said.

"Why?"

"So I can remember you."

"Why do I need to be remembered?" She was blushing now. They'd been together for a year and every day, he still made her blush.

"You know, LA in the fall… who am I to compete against a movie star?" he teased.

"I'll tell them that I'm spoken for," she responded.

He smiled wide. After they finished their Cokes, he asked, "Does the lady wish for supper?"

"Only the finest burgers in Santa Barbara will do," she said, mimicking the poshness of movie stars.

"Then your chariot awaits."

He picked her up and took her in his arms.

The music continued, but the scene faded back into a Technicolor blur. She tried to hold onto the scene, to be Marilou. Something about this life just felt *right*.

She lingered in the between, seeing the stars and the celestial pathway until the guide prompted her to explore a significant moment.

It came clearly, suddenly.

. . .

SHE LOOKED OUT THE WINDOW, at the gently flapping waves. Siren's Cove was more than just a diner—it was Marilou's own beach cottage, one that made her think of the place she and Luke would live one day.

"What are you thinking about?" he asked her from across the table.

"I wish you were coming with me," Marilou said. "To LA."

"You know I would if not for my mom," Luke replied.

"Of course," Marilou said, blushing. "I shouldn't have even said anything. It was selfish and inappropriate to even bring it up."

Luke just smiled. "Last I checked, I have a car, and I think you're going to love living there. Give it six months and you'll be in wardrobe on *Star Trek*."

Marilou lit up at the thought. "That would be nice." She looked down at her burger and took another slow bite. She savored every piece of it—every little bit of the meat, cheese, lettuce and ketchup. Everything about this moment was perfect: the doo-wop music, the scent of ocean air floating in from the diner's open windows, the kitschy decor, and most importantly, the way her beloved Luke looked at her.

"Hey, what do you want to do for your birthday?" Luke asked her. "You only turn eighteen once."

"That's right," Marilou said. "You know, I haven't been to Sokolov Park since I was a kid. When I threw up. And I never got to ride Elbrus because I was four."

"Then let's do it," Luke said.

Sienna wanted to hold onto the scene, but it faded as quickly as the thought came into her head.

Now, we are going to see how this life ended. Please approach this with peace. If it helps to watch from a distance, you may. If you need to stop, all you need to do is open your eyes. Always remember that you are safe.

Dusk. The view of the sunset from Elbrus had been beautiful. They pulled back into the station, a smile on Marilou's face.

Marilou and Luke exited the coaster hand in hand. They stopped as they looked around. It was seven o'clock. That left four hours to explore the park.

"What else do you want to do?" Luke asked with a smile.

She looked back at the line. It had thinned, now projecting a twenty-five-minute wait. Probably because there was an acrobatics show happening at Swan Lake, a parade soon after, or just because people needed to find food. It would back up again as night fell. "Should we go again? Maybe we'll get front row this time."

Luke hesitated. "Um…"

"We don't have to," Marilou said.

Luke smiled, took her hand, and kissed it. "You go. I'll meet you back here in thirty minutes?"

"Okay," she replied.

Luke had something up his sleeve. She knew it. But

she decided to roll with it. They kissed goodbye and she eagerly got in line.

A young Black family got behind her in line a moment later. The girl was young and wearing a sky-blue dress as she almost smacked into Marilou.

"Careful, baby," the mother said. She turned to Marilou as she gathered her daughter in her arms. "Sorry."

"No problem," Marilou said cheerfully. She turned to the daughter, pointing to her own sky-blue top. "Hey, we match."

The girl smiled.

"What's your name?" she asked.

The girl blushed as she walked back into her father's arms.

"This is Jane," said the father.

"Hi, Jane. I'm Marilou. Are you excited?"

Jane nodded with a smile.

"Is this your first time?"

She nodded again—

—AND ABRUPTLY, Sienna couldn't breathe. She opened her eyes and let out a gasp.

She touched the carpet, the blankets, smelled the candle.

Her name was Sienna Larsen.

It was 2025.

Still, she couldn't stop the heavy breaths.

Gabby sat up, stopped the video, and looked over at Sienna. "What? What was it?"

"You didn't tell me how…" Sienna trailed off, then found her words again. "I think something bad happened to me."

Gabby nodded vaguely. "Oh. Sure. That happens sometimes. I didn't tell you, the time I made gunpowder, someone put a hit out on me. That's how I died."

Sienna laughed dryly, still trying to catch her breath. "Let's not do that again."

"Oh," Gabby said quietly. "I'm sorry."

"No, it's just… it was very real."

THEY MOVED into the kitchen where they had a late lunch of leftover pasta salad that Gabby's mom had made the night before. The girls were quiet as they ate. It hadn't always been like that.

"By the way," Gabby said, breaking a stretch of silence, "your comment about me being a cultist hurt my feelings. I just wanted to say that."

"Sorry," Sienna said. "I was joking."

"Well, it hurt my feelings, okay?"

"Okay, I'm sorry."

"Okay."

The following silence was all-consuming in its awkwardness. For what was probably only a minute but seemed much longer, the only sounds were the clinking of their forks, the tapping of their water glasses on the counter and the whir of the air conditioner. Then, Gabby asked Sienna if she was busy next weekend.

"No," Sienna said. "Why?"

"I want to go to that new park and I'm trying to find someone to go with that's not my parents."

"New park?" Sienna asked.

"Well it's not new, I think. It just reopened," Gabby explained.

"Oh," Sienna said, feeling her heart begin to thump. "What's it called?"

"Shoot, I can't think of it," Gabby said. "It's on the tip of my tongue… it's in Chino Hills, though."

Sokolov. She's talking about Sokolov. "Is that the one where the roller coaster derailed?"

"Oh," Gabby said. "I don't know. Well, do you wanna go?"

"I'll have to see," Sienna said quietly. Her heart was racing fast again.

"Hey, you could invite Josh," Gabby offered.

"No," Sienna replied with a blush. "We're not really talking right now."

"What? Why?"

"I don't know, I asked him to tell me about his trip and it's mostly been radio silence since," Sienna said.

She used to have such a crush on him, and everyone thinking they were a thing only caused it to grow. One time, during her James Bond phase, they'd gone to a screening of *Goldfinger* at the local theater. He'd walked her home.

"They just don't make them like they used to," Sienna told him as they approached her house.

Josh had smiled at her in such a way that made her feel truly wanted for the first time in her entire life. "You are one of a kind," he'd told her. They'd stopped at her doorway and were facing each other.

"Oh?"

She thought they were going to kiss—and then they didn't.

Gabby's comment brought her back. "When are you two going to be real and finally admit that you like each other?"

"I don't know. I'm not inviting him," Sienna said.

"Okay," Gabby said in a sardonic tone. "Suit yourself." It lingered in the air.

SIENNA'S HEAD was still spinning by the time she got home. Her mother was in the living room, reading a magazine.

"How was Gabby's?" she asked.

"Fine," Sienna whispered.

"It's nice that you two stay in touch," her mother said.

"Yeah," Sienna replied. She needed to finish that video.

Her mother stopped her. "Burgers for dinner tonight?"

No. Literally anything but. "It's too hot for burgers," Sienna said.

"Alright, then what do you want?"

"I'm not hungry," Sienna replied.

"Well, if you get hungry, don't come crying to me."

"Okay." Please—not now. Her mother needed to leave so she could finish the video. "Can I watch something?"

In response, Sienna's mother stood up, handed her the remote, and moved into the kitchen. Once she was occupied with... dishes, it seemed like, Sienna turned on the TV, opened YouTube, and picked up the video where she'd left off.

With the scene now set, the essayist began with a virtual tour of sorts, one that was delicately and meticulously constructed from pictures, ads, and scans of park maps.

An enormous, hand-carved sign greeted guests at the entrance, just before their cars turned up a tree-lined road. The theming had already begun before anyone even entered the park. It was popular. People wanted to go.

She'd wanted to go.

She'd thrown up there as a kid. That's why it was all so familiar.

About halfway in, the video's tone shifted to one of foreboding.

In the 1960s, both Dmitri Sokolov and his park fell on hard times. In 1962, Ivan Kozlov, his lead engineer since the beginning, questioned the lack of maintenance inspections. He was promptly fired. Desperate to cut costs wherever he could, Sokolov hired teenagers to run the park's day-to-day operations. They weren't trained. There was no one to supervise them. More than that, they didn't question anything. These facts were well-hidden from the public until after the investigation. After all, Sokolov's goal was to keep the park running, and earn whatever money he could on the dream he'd sunk his life into.

Until August 12th, 1967, he'd done just that.

Before discussing the incident, the essayist called for a moment of silence for the victims. He mentioned some of the injured first. Anna Lawrence, thirteen, was paralyzed from the waist down. Her brother James, sixteen, sitting next to her, developed debilitating chronic pain and was forced to abandon his dream of becoming an Olympic swimmer. The were just two out of twenty-eight on that fateful Elbrus ride who escaped with their lives but not without lifelong scars.

Then, the dead.

Teddy Hawkins, seventeen, a budding chemist with a bright future, was in the wrong place at the wrong time. The whole family was at the park that day—him, his mother, plus his father and sister. When the time came for them to get in line for Elbrus, his mother Sandra was tired and didn't want to ride. So, Teddy waited with her on a nearby bench. When the coaster derailed from the track and barreled right towards them, he had to act fast. While he'd saved his mother, Teddy had not been so lucky.

The two front rows of the car had been completely crushed when they'd careened into the ground. From a height of fifty feet, the people in them didn't have a chance.

Walter Keppel, thirty-seven, was an insurance agent from Los Angeles. He was there with his wife, Cynthia, thirty-five, and their daughter, Jane, eight...

The family... it was them.

Sweet Jane...

Sienna knew what was coming before it did.

Marilou Chambers, eighteen. The fresh high school graduate was celebrating her birthday with her boyfriend and was set to attend UCLA in the fall. She dreamed of working as a costume designer for film and TV.

The joy on Marilou's face radiated through the TV screen.

How did she know…

How had she seen it all so clearly?

Shaking, Sienna stopped the video.

She'd never even heard about this incident before today, and yet, it was changing her. The meditation was only one small part of it.

Sienna's mother came into the living room, noticing the TV screen. "What are you watching?"

"Nothing," Sienna said.

"That girl kind of looks like you," her mother replied. She looked again. "Actually, she totally does."

Sienna felt her stomach turn. "I guess. I don't really see it."

Her mother sighed. "So, any more thoughts on dinner?"

"Anything but burgers," Sienna replied.

"I'll make pad thai, how about that?"

"Sure," Sienna said. "Hey mom, do you remember when I threw up at a theme park as a kid? Where were we?"

Sienna's mother stared blankly at her daughter. "I don't remember that. And believe me, I would have."

"Are you sure?" she said, continuing to look at Marilou's photo on the TV screen. "Was it this place called Sokolov Park?"

"Sienna," her mother said. "Sokolov's been closed since I was little."

"Oh," she replied. "I suddenly started remembering a time I got really sick at a park when I was a kid. I'm just trying to remember where it happened because I think that's when I started hating roller coasters."

"Probably Disney," Sienna's mother said before she disappeared into the kitchen.

It wasn't Disney. She knew that for sure. But she let it go for now.

Still paused, Sienna scrolled through the comments, each offering their opinions on what victim's story they found the most tragic.

my heart breaks for that poor eight-year-old.

The girl's boyfriend who didn't ride with her . . . so tragic. it's disgusting this park didn't immediately shutter.

The one that wasn't even on the coaster and protecting his mom....

One made her heart pound especially fast.

I went to high school with Marilou Chambers and Luke Krieger. Both so nice. Luke was never the same after this.

Marilou. She had a life. People that knew her, knew Luke...

It wasn't just her imagination.

Sienna looked at the run time. She had twelve minutes left. Might as well power through.

There was an investigation and a trial, one that revealed the extent of Elbrus's maintenance issues. Experts testified that it was only a matter of time before disaster struck. Sokolov had been warned—by Ivan Kozlov, by others—but he ignored them all. He was arrested and charged with manslaughter.

The video flashed black-and-white photos from throughout the trial. One particularly stirring one depicted a young survivor, his face bruised, his neck and both arms in casts. Yet the fire, passion, and determination in his eyes was evident.

In the front row of the audience, a distraught middle-aged couple held up a picture of Marilou. They looked nothing like Sienna's parents. And Sienna was certain her parents never shared a loving embrace like these two did. Still, looking at them stirred a sense of familiarity, pain and regret all at once within her.

The video cut back to an image of Sokolov himself. Sienna shook her body and forced herself to continue watching.

Found guilty of five counts of second-degree involuntary manslaughter, Sokolov sobbed about how all he ever wanted was to bring joy to people's lives. He was sentenced to five years and served less than two. Most commenters agreed that this was a travesty. One commenter who expressed that they felt bad for Sokolov was promptly piled on.

In spite of his imprisonment, the park continued running as his eldest son took over operations. Still, it would never recover and it closed in 1977. Sokolov himself lived in anonymity and died two years later.

That was that, until Sokolov's grandson decided to sink millions of dollars into rebuilding the park, buying back the land after becoming a tech billionaire in his own right.

In response to the predictable backlash, he'd said, "My grandfather gave countless people happy lifelong memories for sixteen years. And it's all been reduced to one bad day. His legacy should be more than that. And if you don't like it, don't come."

The essayist closed by mentioning that the park was set to reopen on June 13th, 2025 and asked commenters to chime in with their thoughts. As Sienna read through them again, the responses were mixed. Some thought the park was a gravesite and should be left alone. Others welcomed the opportunity to build a new chapter not defined by tragedy.

Sienna saw that the video was from April. It was now August. That meant the park must have been up and running for about two months. She took out her phone and googled, "Sokolov Park Reopening"

Sure enough, she saw the operating hours. It had indeed been going on quietly since June. It was a scaled back version of the park. No Elbrus, obviously, but it had everything else that people had always loved about it. The lake. The circus tent. The shows.

She supposed that she didn't see the harm.

THAT NIGHT, she dreamt she was inside a massive circus tent. The ground had been paved for dancing. The scent of buttered popcorn and cotton candy was potent as she scanned her surroundings, looking for someone she knew. Old-timey music filled the space.

"Took you long enough," came a boy's voice. Teddy Hawkins, thin and boyish. He looked at her with a serious face.

"I'm sorry," she whispered.

"They've got a special place roped off for us," he said. "No need to wait in line."

The Keppels were waiting for them in the back room. Jane was eating a stick of cotton candy, and her parents were smiling as they watched.

SIENNA WOKE WITH A SWEAT.

It was just a dream.

A dream because the park had been on her mind. That's all.

A ding came through on her phone. It was her mother.

> at work today — there's cereal for breakfast and you can make a pb&j for lunch.

Sienna didn't reply. She looked at her weather app again. High of 110 today. That was practically a cold front.

The dream lingered in her mind as she sat up in bed.

Sienna clicked out of the article and went back to Google. Next: "Marilou Chambers." That gave her nothing. But "Marilou Chambers Sokolov Park" did.

The first search result yielded Wikipedia's article about the Sokolov Park Disaster. The second was Marilou's memorial page, preserved on a website stuck in the 1990s.

She clicked.

Marilou Mildred Chambers
August 12th, 1949 — August 12th, 1967

A quote was below it.

```
"I'm    a    romantic;    a    sentimental
person  thinks  things  will  last,  a
romantic  person  hopes  against  hope
that they won't."
   ~ F. Scott Fitzgerald
```

This Side of Paradise. Her—no, Marilou's—favorite book. She knew it even before she read the description that confirmed it. But that detail spooked her out less than it would have a day before.

Marilou was a straight-A student. She loved reading, movies, traveling, and adventure. It was that spirit that made her want to celebrate her birthday at Sokolov.

She had a perfect family and a perfect boyfriend. Did this girl have any flaws at all? Sienna kind of hated Marilou.

Sienna scrolled to look at the pictures. A grainy one stirred something within Sienna. In the first she posed alongside Yucca trees. She knew that she'd never been to Joshua Tree, but she looked at them with a same familiarity as a place she'd experienced many times before.

She looked up Luke next.

Information about him was scant, save his obituary. 1987. He'd had a heart attack at thirty-eight.

Next, she Googled: "are past lives real?" AI summaries of different articles were inconclusive. She sighed, clicked out of the search, took a deep breath, and texted Gabby.

> I'm in for Sokolov.

Whatever was happening, whatever was triggering it, she was being pulled to this place like a magnet. She knew there was no stopping it. She sent another text.

> Also send me the meditation

Gabby replied.

Sienna wrote back.

> Just do it please.

A moment later, Gabby sent the link.

After breakfast, Sienna went back into her room. She lit a candle called "Watermelon Summer." It was $3 and from Walmart. Not exactly crystals, but it would do.

THE SECOND TIME on the celestial bridge, Sienna moved with intention, knowing that she would once again access Marilou's reality.

She didn't even know what her goal was this time. Even for a little while, she just wanted to live in a reality where everything made sense, where everything went her way.

From the moment Sienna felt her hands against the cool brass once again, she'd become Marilou.

The first scene was of some sort of outdoor barbecue. She sat on a picnic bench, smelled smoked meat, and let the aftertaste of Cherry Coke sit on her tongue. The glass bottle was next to her.

She smiled at her father, grilling burgers close by. A boy—her young cousin—spooked her with a dinosaur-like roar.

"I got you!" Petey exclaimed.

"You got me!" Marilou exclaimed back.

He was in the midst of telling her about a fantasy world he wanted her to participate in alongside the rest of the cousins when she heard her father's voice.

"Lucas, hot dog or burger?"

"Burger, please."

She didn't see Luke until he sat and put his arm around her.

Petey got Luke's attention now and regaled him with tales of this fantasy world.

As Marilou beamed, Sienna's thoughts broke through.

I've never known...

... this.

THE SIGNIFICANT EVENT took her back to 1966. She and Luke were lying in her room, arm in arm as sunlight flooded through her lace curtains. It gave The Beatles and The Beach Boys posters on her walls and the hot-pink tapestry opposite her bed a soft glow. She had his head on her shoulder as they sat in the moment, taking in the faint sea breeze outside the window. As his lips caressed hers, the more he gave, the more she needed.

As his kisses moved to her neck and shoulder, the pleasure she felt was so intense she had to pull away.

Her face was bright red as she looked at Luke and he looked back at her. "What is it?" he said.

"Not until we're married?" Marilou said.

"Okay," Luke said, taking her hand and smiling as he kissed each individual finger. "We'll wait. I love you."

"I love you too," Marilou replied.

It was the first time they'd ever exchanged those words.

"I do really want to kiss you, though," Luke said.

"I never said anything about kissing."

As he brought his lips to hers, Sienna lived in the feeling for as long as possible. She knew what was coming next.

So what if she'd died on her eighteenth birthday?

Marilou Chambers had everything she'd ever wanted in life.

If being perfect meant you died young, maybe that was an alright trade…

Speaking of…

She was called once again, to see how her life ended.

This time, she wasn't going to have a panic attack. No matter what it took, she was determined to see it through to the very end.

THE KEPPELS GOT in line behind her not long after she'd decided to ride Elbrus a second time.

From the moment Marilou told Jane the two of them matched, they were fast friends. "Jane, I want to know all about your day."

Jane blushed.

Cynthia, the mother, smiled. "She's talking to you, Janey."

"We got here right when they opened at eight, and we went on The Wolverine and Serbian Wilds, but my favorite part was the Swan Boats," Jane excitedly told her.

"My boyfriend and I just did those earlier. We probably walked right by each other and didn't even know it."

Jane smiled. The line was moving quickly. The foliage covering the lattice work, barrels laid out with vintage mountain climbing gear—it was all immaculate.

"I've never been to Europe," she told Jane. "But this roller coaster is pretty fun. And you are so brave."

"She's a daredevil," Walter said. "Don't know where she gets it from."

Jane took two steps towards Marilou.

"Jane, do you think we're going to get front row? I really hope so."

Jane nodded eagerly. "Where's your boyfriend?" she asked.

"Oh, well, he's a poopyhead and didn't want to ride again," Marilou told her. She leaned down and whispered to Jane like she was letting her in on a secret. "I think he's too scared."

"How old are you?" Jane asked.

"Today's my birthday. I'm eighteen."

"Happy birthday, sweetheart," Cynthia said.

"I don't think anything's going to beat the time I saw The Beatles," Marilou said. "But it's been a perfect day."

By the time they'd reached the queue, Marilou practically had a job lined up to babysit Jane when she moved to LA in the fall.

Jane took Marilou's hand and gave it a tight squeeze as

they watched the car pull into the station and saw its riders get off. She was shaking.

"What's wrong? Are you scared?" Marilou asked.

Jane shook her head.

"That's the cool thing about roller coasters. They're fun because they seem scary, all while they keep us safe."

Cynthia and Walter watched the two with a smile as the ride operator got Marilou's attention, gesturing towards the front row.

"Two in your party?" the operator asked.

Marilou looked back at Jane's parents.

"You want to go up with her in the front, baby?" Cynthia asked.

Jane nodded, and Marilou continued to hold her hand as they approached.

"Come on, mountain climber!" she exclaimed as the two got in the cart.

Once they sat, Sienna felt the memory fading, the urge to wake up.

No.

She had to stay in it.

Cynthia and Walter got in the seats behind them. Jane, the daredevil, was shaking.

"Are you okay?" Marilou asked.

Jane nodded as the ride operator came to lower their safety bars.

"See," Marilou told her. "We're not going anywhere."

Cynthia caught eyes with her then. "Thank you," she whispered.

A moment later, they were ascending the first lift hill.

Jane gripped her bar tightly as Marilou took in the perfect summer evening.

She had a beautiful view of the park, the surrounding city, and the sinking streaks of pink in the sky from up here. She could only wonder what it must be like to actually climb a mountain.

They got to the top. "Here we go!" Marilou told Jane.

Jane held on for the first drop as Marilou lifted her arms up into the sky. Both girls were smiling once they were on flat track again. But not for long. "Wasn't that fun?" she whispered.

"Yeah!" Jane exclaimed.

The second lift hill came then, and with it, Sienna's urge to open her eyes.

No.

Stay.

Marilou lifted her arms, and Jane followed.

The second drop was pure bliss for them both.

They were approaching the loop now, the one where they would go upside down. "You ready? It's really fun!"

Jane nodded excitedly.

They went up. Then upside down and back down. As they ascended the gentle lift hill, both were smiling. This was thrill, this was happiness—it was everything.

Marilou noticed the crowd of people in the night, wondering if Luke was somewhere among them, waiting for her. The last thing she saw was fireworks in the night sky.

. . .

SIENNA OPENED HER EYES, breathing heavily.

Fuck!

Back to her room and her sad, boring life.

She rubbed her eyes, wondering why all of this was happening to her now.

She'd never heard of Marilou Chambers, Luke Krieger, or Sokolov Park before yesterday.

She wanted to tell somebody, but who? Definitely not Josh. Not Gabby, not yet. Her mother wouldn't understand.

Maybe she would tell Gabby and take the "I told you so."

Or maybe Gabby would look at her like she was crazy.

To anyone else, what would she say? "I used to be a perfect girl with a perfect boyfriend until I died in a roller coaster accident and now I'm stuck with my shitty life."

No, she'd wait and say something when she and Gabby went to the park, but only if it came up on its own.

For the rest of the week, Sienna thought little of Marilou or of Sokolov Park.

She'd gone down a googling rabbit hole, but didn't uncover much else except someone selling a park map from the 1960s for over $100,000.

Whatever she was looking for, she knew she wouldn't find it until she went back.

THEY WENT ON SATURDAY, August 10th—the first day the temperatures sunk into the double digits. It would still be a high of 97, but Sienna and Gabby packed their swimsuits to take advantage of the park's waterslides. If that wasn't enough, she thought they'd have to take frequent breaks in the air conditioning.

After about forty-five minutes of driving, it was late morning and they were getting close. There was no sign indicating the park was nearby and they had to go off the GPS alone.

Sienna looked at the map. It wanted them to turn in another three quarters of a mile. But the turn they were approaching—one that went up a tree-lined hill—was the one. "Turn here," she said.

"Are you sure?" Gabby asked.

"Yes," Sienna insisted.

Gabby skeptically got into the turn lane.

As they snaked up the road, Gabby kept asking if she was sure this was it. There were no other cars. No signs.

But Sienna knew this was the way.

"You think it would be better marked," Gabby said once Sienna knew they were getting close.

"They don't want to draw attention to it because of the backlash, I guess," Sienna said.

Gabby was skeptical until the moment they pulled into the parking lot. There was a decent crowd there, and they saw a heavily backed up line of cars coming from the other direction. The way the GPS had told them to go...

Sienna's heart skipped a beat as they pulled into a spot. The ticket booth, fashioned to look like a woodland cabin, beckoned to her.

"You're so quiet," Gabby said.

"Yeah... I... thanks for thinking of this."

"Sure, don't mention it," she said.

As they got out of the car and both lathered up with sunscreen, Sienna's eyes caught the many people doing the same around her. It might not have been anything like it once was, but there was still a decent crowd. Maybe none of this was as big of a deal as the internet made it seem.

Sienna quickened her pace towards the ticket booth, wanting to move towards the sound of old-timey carnival music coming from within.

"Hey, wait up!" Gabby shouted.

Sienna stopped.

"What's with you?" she said, catching up. "You were wishy-washy about coming, then you agreed. You've had nothing to say all morning, then you somehow know about a secret shortcut to a place you've never been to before. Now you can't wait to get inside?"

Sienna let out a deep sigh. She wanted to tell Gabby, but where would she even begin? She knew she'd get her answers as soon as they were in the park. Only then would she broach it.

Tickets granting them unlimited access were thirty dollars a person. Adjusted for inflation, that was the cost of entry back in its heyday, the teenage boy operating the booth explained. He told them to enjoy their visit in a monotone voice.

Only one family was in line in front of them as they entered through the gates.

It was so... quiet. And Sokolov Park had never been that.

They were transported to a Russian village at the dawn of the twentieth century, in those few years before the 1905 Revolution, before the rise of Vladimir Lenin. It was a place built on the memories of Dmitri Sokolov's childhood.

They'd go on The Wolverine first, get a ride in, come back to shop and then figure out what else they wanted to do.

IN ITS HEYDAY, as a gentler, simpler ride, The Wolverine always existed in Elbrus's shadow. But it was still here and the other one wasn't. Sienna couldn't help but stare at the large painted image of its mascot and remember that this *was* the original sign. Redone, of course, but this is what people would have seen in 1967. The original ride track, too.

There were about five people in line and as such, Sienna barely had time to process that she was actually doing this before the ride operators were were calling her and Gabby forward.

Still, by the time it was done, she was smiling. "That was more fun than I remember," she said as they exited.

As Gabby stared at her blankly, Sienna felt her face flush.

"I meant, than I thought it would be."

Gabby said nothing, and they continued about their day.

. . .

BY ELEVEN O'CLOCK, they'd gotten in line to see an escape artist in the circus tent. The line went outside and around the enormous structure. The pictures hadn't done its grandeur justice. In that moment, she ached for the park that had been lost on that terrible day. This really had been a place of joy. It must have been.

A moment later, they were ushered inside to a red and gold waiting room and a series of giant fans. Sienna instantly made a beeline for one. She and Gabby exchanged a laugh as her blouse flew up in the air like a parachute around her waist. She looked down, then up and suddenly—

—THE SPACE WAS FILLED with at least a hundred people. It wasn't Gabby smiling at her, it was Luke. He extended his hand, which she took with a smile as he moved her away from the fan.

A staff member dressed as a circus attendant got everyone's attention. Soon, the escape artist would be ready for them, but they needed to line up in order to be admitted. The chaos of shifting bodies and quickening paces was overwhelming. As they tried to find their place in line, families kept shoving in front of them. They'd finally settled close to the exit when Marilou turned to Luke with an eye-roll.

"Jeez," she remarked.

Before he could respond, a guest standing behind them cleared his throat. "Eh-hem."

Neither said anything.

The guest tapped Marilou's shoulder. "Hey, I'm talking to you," he said.

They both turned, seeing that he was a boy around their age as they caught his thin frame and accusing stare.

"It's rude to cut in line," the boy said.

Marilou noticed his family then. His younger sister—probably about fifteen—was glaring at them, but the parents were too busy talking about something to realize what was going on. "Sorry," she told him. "It was a little bit chaotic."

As he and the sister continued to glare, Marilou gave Luke a look, gesturing towards the end of the line. *This isn't worth it,* her eyes told him.

He didn't listen. "It's rude to be rude to my girlfriend on her birthday," he snapped.

"Luke—" Marilou started.

"I didn't realize your birthday gave you permission to cut in line," the boy said.

"It doesn't," Marilou muttered. "I'm sorry, we made a mistake…"

"No, we did not," Luke insisted, raising his eyebrow. "Why don't you mind your own business?"

"Hey!" the boy yelled towards a nearby staff member. When they turned and looked in his direction, he continued, "some help over here?"

Others around them were staring.

Marilou and Luke took that as their cue to give up and found their way to the very back.

"Jerk," Marilou said.

"Don't let him get to you," Luke told her with a reassuring rub of her shoulder.

"EARTH TO SIENNA!" Gabby's voice called.

They were opening the doors to let people in.

Sienna shook the memory off as she joined her friend.

"You were like, completely spaced out," Gabby told her.

"Yeah, I know," Sienna muttered.

The show was about the begin. She needed a distraction.

ABOUT HALFWAY THROUGH THE SHOW, she'd completely forgotten about the bizarre memory. Anyways, what could she do about it?

The escape artist had started off with small tricks. He'd just presented the audience with a cage. He was explaining that he was going to go inside, lock himself in, and then get out when a voice called in her ear, loud and biting.

"Why do you get another shot? I came back as an ant. An ant! Can you believe it?"

It was Teddy.

Sienna wanted to tell him that didn't seem half bad, but he kept berating her.

"I was exterminated by some Karen who didn't want me in her home. That's what I get for saving my mom. Who did you save, Marilou? Oh—no one. You lied to that little girl!"

"It wasn't my fault!" she shouted. Suddenly, everyone's eyes were on her, the escape artist included.

If Sienna thought she'd known embarrassment before, this was next level.

Gabby stood up, led her outside and to the nearest bench.

"What wasn't your fault?" she asked.

Sienna knew she was going to have to explain everything now. "That past life… the meditation…I *died* here. When the coaster derailed."

Gabby laughed wryly. "Girl, you know that's all just for fun, right?"

"Is it, though?"

"What do you mean?" Gabby asked.

"I've had visions… things I can't explain… and when I asked you to send me the link, I become a girl… Marilou Chambers… she was *real*. People knew her and she had a boyfriend that looked just like Josh and people knew him too… And…" She caught her breath, unable to find the words. "I think she was me. I really do."

Gabby just stared.

"Anyways, let's just have fun. I just want to have fun here."

"Okay," she said quietly.

Although the day passed without incident until mid-afternoon, neither girl had much to say to each other. They were walking past the swan boats when Gabby finally said, "So, in your visions, you hear talking and everything?"

"I hear, I taste, I smell... I don't know how I could just make any of this up."

"My visions have never been that clear," Gabby said. "It's like I'm watching a movie."

"For me... I feel like I *am* Marilou."

By then, they were approaching a serene field filled with multicolored flowers. There were benches and pathways all leading to a water fountain.

Sienna stopped in her tracks. "This is where Elbrus used to be."

"How do you know?" Gabby said. She caught herself a second later.

Sienna didn't speak. She just continued, one foot in front of the other, until—

"You belong here with us, Marilou."

"Leave me alone, Teddy!" Sienna shrieked.

Nearby guests stared. Gabby just gave them a "nothing to see here" look and once again, led Sienna to the nearest bench.

Once they were sitting, Sienna cupped her face in her hands and cried, only for Teddy to taunt her again.

"You know it's true."

I've Been Here Before

THE NIGHT SKY was beautiful even before the fireworks graced it.

Earlier in the day, they'd been walking by the fair games close to Swan Lake. Marilou's eye had caught a giant teddy bear, a yellow one with adorable beady eyes and matching bow around its neck. It reminded her of one she had as a kid, one that had gotten lost on a trip to Colorado.

"Oh, isn't he beautiful?" she told Luke.

"I think I've got to win that for you," he said.

That's why he didn't come. He was getting it for her.

Her body warmed at the thought of seeing him in just a few short minutes. She looked back at Jane and the two exchanged smiles. Then, back at the track, and the station out of the corner of her eye.

But they weren't turning left. They were going right, off the tracks, from fifty feet in the air.

Marilou heard the screams—from Cynthia, from everyone in the cars behind them. But it happened too fast and too slow all at once for her to do the same.

As they barreled towards a bench and a mother and son who just happened to be sitting there, she heard the mother cry out first. Then, she got a good look at the son just as Jane fell into her arms.

The boy from the circus tent—

He pushed his mother out of the way just as the car crashed right into him.

The mother wailed, and Marilou heard the boy's name.

Teddy.

She looked back at Jane, peacefully lying against her side, almost as if she was asleep.

A few rows behind them, a boy and girl were screaming and crying. Marilou knew they were in agony.

She didn't feel much of anything at all.

Her dying thoughts were of Luke, the teddy bear, and standing on the bridge of the Enterprise, carrying the famous uniforms on hangers as she waited to meet William Shatner.

Then it was back to the stars, to peace.

THE NEXT THING SIENNA KNEW, Gabby was sitting beside her, gently rubbing her back.

"I told that little girl she was safe," Sienna said through sobs. "I saw the boy as we crashed into him… and Luke… he was going to surprise me with a teddy bear."

"Do you want to leave?" Gabby asked.

"Just wait. Let's live in it a little longer," Sienna whispered.

They stayed at the park until mid-afternoon, riding the rides, having turkey rice bowls for lunch—those were new—and coming back to the fountain so Sienna could throw a penny into the well. As she was fishing one out of her wallet, she saw the bronze plaque. There wasn't much except five names and a sentence-long acknowledgment of the disaster, but it was enough.

Just before Sienna closed her eyes, she noticed Gabby was doing the same thing.

I want my life to make sense for once, Sienna thought.

She watched as the penny flicked against the water's surface and sank downward with all the other ones. Then she looked to Gabby, watching hers. "Let me guess. You wished for world peace."

"Yeah," was all Gabby said. "We need it."

They were ready to go after that.

THE NEXT MORNING, Sienna got the best sleep she'd had in a while. Her hand moved to her phone, looking at the text she'd drafted to Josh. It took a few seconds, but she forced herself to press send and put it out of her mind.

A few minutes later, his response came through.

> hey, sounds good! Tomorrow work for you?

She replied.

> Absolutely

acknowledgments

The process of putting this book together has been a strange and beautiful process of exploration.

Thank you to my beta readers, for helping shape these stories.

Olivia Bennett, for making them the best they could be.

To who read and loved them as individual pieces, for inspiring me to keep going.

Amanda McKnight, Katrina Lenk, Broghanne Jessamine, Kat Bohn and Tavish Grade, for bringing them to life in audio, and Ben Johnson, for your beautiful compositions.

To everyone still here, I am honored and humbled you would choose to spend your time engaging with my work. Thank you—sincerely—for listening for what I have to say.

about the author

Eleanor Wells is a writer, filmmaker, and actress, born and raised in Milwaukee, Wisconsin. She graduated from Emerson College in 2017 with a BA in Media Arts Production. She resides in Los Angeles, California and is the author of *All Our Yesterdays*.

www.ingramcontent.com/pod-product-compliance
Lightning Source LLC
LaVergne TN
LVHW041610070526
838199LV00052B/3075